Jenny Oldfield

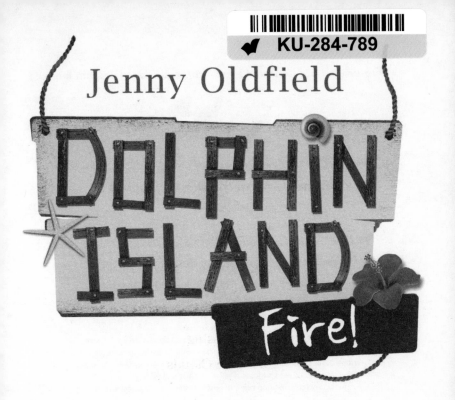

DOLPHIN ISLAND

Fire!

Illustrations by
Daniel Howarth

Hodder
Children's
Books

For lovely Lola, Jude and Evan – three dedicated dolphin fans

HODDER CHILDREN'S BOOKS

First published in Great Britain in 2018 by Hodder and Stoughton

1 3 5 7 9 10 8 6 4 2

Text copyright © Jenny Oldfield, 2018

Inside illustrations copyright © Daniel Howarth, 2018

The moral rights of the author and illustrator have been asserted.

A CIP catalogue record for this book is available from the British Library.

ISBN 978 1 444 92830 3

Typeset in ITC Caslon 224

Printed and bound in Great Britain by Clays Ltd, St Ives plc

The paper and board used in this book are made from wood
from responsible sources.

Hodder Children's Books
An imprint of Hachette Children's Group
Part of Hodder and Stoughton
Carmelite House
50 Victoria Embankment
London EC4Y 0DZ

An Hachette UK Company
www.hachette.co.uk

www.hachettechildrens.co.uk

Chapter One

'Day 27.' Six-year-old Mia Fisher made another notch in the calendar stick.

'That means we've been here for almost four weeks,' her older sister, Fleur, said with a long sigh.

Four weeks marooned on Dolphin Island felt like for ever. Gone from their world were streets and houses, cars and shops. Instead they had sand and palm trees, restless waves and blue skies. And dolphins. Of course – how could Fleur forget about the dolphins? She shook herself then looked eagerly out to sea in the hope of catching sight of Jazz, Stormy and Pearl.

The sun had just risen. Gentle waves lapped at the rocky headlands and the sea sparkled on for ever. But there was no sign of their special dolphin friends.

Mia and Fleur's brother, Alfie, came out of the

shelter carrying the watch that he'd salvaged from the *Kestrel* wreck. The small yacht belonging to two unknown sailors had sunk close to the shore during a recent storm.

Mia took it from him then held it to her ear. Quickly she handed it back. 'Listen to that – it makes a ticking noise.' Her brown hair was tightly braided, her face freckled and tanned.

Alfie grinned. 'That's because it's not digital. It's an old-fashioned watch that you have to wind up,' he explained.

'The kind that Granddad Tony wears,' Fleur added.

A frown appeared on Mia's face. 'I miss him and Gran,' she whispered.

'We all do,' Fleur said sadly. She remembered the last time they'd seen them, standing in the airport to wave them off. That was the day in July when they'd flown out to Australia with their mum and dad then set off from Queensland in their granddad's yacht, *Merlin* – at the start of their big adventure, before the tropical storm that had wrecked their boat and cast them away on Dolphin Island. 'But don't worry – we'll see them again soon.'

'When?' Mia asked.

'When we get rescued.'

'When?'

'Soon.' Fleur gave Mia a quick hug. 'I'll tell you what: who wants to come and look for birds' eggs for breakfast?'

'Me!' Mia jumped at the chance. She skipped and hopped towards the cliff behind the shelter.

'What about you?' Fleur asked Alfie.

'Nope.' He slipped the watch into his pocket then patted the knife tucked inside the waistband of his red swimming shorts. Then he set off across the white sand. 'I'm planning to cut down more bamboo on Turtle Beach.'

The bamboo was for the new raft that their mum and dad had started to build. They wanted to make it stronger and better than the one Alfie had used when he'd set out alone to explore what lay off the southern tip of the island. He'd almost drowned, so this time there would be no going off on solo voyages.

'OK, see you at breakfast.' Fleur had to hurry to catch up with Mia, who was scrambling up the cliff path like one of the monkeys who lived in the forest. She was like a little monkey herself – nimble and surefooted, but easier to spot in her turquoise swimmie. 'Wait for me!' Fleur yelled after her.

Just then their mum, Katie, emerged from the shelter. 'Hats!' she reminded them.

So Fleur had to back-track and grab the two home-made sunhats that her mum presented to her. They were woven out of strips of palm leaf. Mia's first hat had blown away during a hurricane so Fleur had made her a new one, complete with bright red and yellow feathers sticking out of the band that held it together. 'Thanks,' she gasped then raced off up the cliff path.

James Fisher followed Katie out of the shelter. He'd just got up and was rubbing sleep from his eyes. 'Someone's feeling better,' he remarked to his wife as he watched Fleur scale the cliff.

'Yes, thank heavens.' A week earlier their eldest daughter had been laid low with tick-bite fever. She'd been so weak that she hadn't been able to stand and there had been a worry that she might not survive. 'And thanks to Jazz, Pearl and Stormy too.'

Meanwhile, Fleur and Mia carried on up the cliff path. Fleur was glad to be back in action after being so poorly and was, as ever, on the lookout for their friendly dolphins. 'Jazz, where are you?' she said out loud as she paused to look down at the blue water. 'You kept me company while I was sick. Now I want to let you know that I'm better.'

Mia had scrambled on ahead. 'What did you say?' she yelled over her shoulder as a breeze blew strands of hair across her sticky cheeks.

'Nothing. Carry on.'

'Who were you talking to?'

'No one. I said, let's carry on.' *Jazz, where are you?* Fleur thought with another long sigh.

'Fibber!' Mia challenged with a cheeky grin. 'You were talking to Jazz, and he's not even here!'

'OK, I admit it.' Through storm and shipwreck, Jazz, Stormy and Pearl had stayed by the side of the Fisher family. The dolphins had protected them since the day when *Merlin* had sunk – they'd played alongside them and even taught them how to catch fish.

'Hah!' Mia's grin widened. 'You were talking to

Mr Nobody!'

   'So?' Fleur said with a shrug. *Come on, Jazz, pay me a visit!* The ocean was calm and completely empty. It was days since they'd spied a passing ship or even a plane flying overhead, and it was only the company of their faithful dolphins that had kept the family going.

   'Eggs!' Mia reminded her brightly. 'Come on,

slowcoach – I'm hungry!'

Fleur climbed with Mia until they came to Butterfly Falls. Here, she took off her hat and turned it upside down. 'We can store the eggs in here, if we find any,' she suggested.

*

Mia counted eggs as they placed them in the hat.

'... Three, four, five. Is that enough?'

'No, that's only one each and gannets' eggs aren't very big.' Fleur decided they had to go on searching the crevices in the rock where the birds laid their eggs. But first she wanted to cool her feet in the stream. She sat on a boulder and dipped them in the clear water, taking time to notice an orange butterfly resting on a broad, shiny leaf that overhung the waterfall. There were five black spots on each of its brightly coloured wings.

Mia plonked herself down beside Fleur. The startled butterfly took flight. But there was plenty of other nature stuff for Fleur to look at – she spotted three white cockatoos perched in a bush, squawking and making an almighty din, with their yellow crests raised in anger at the human interruption. Better still, she spied a cane toad squatting on a wet rock at the edge of the waterfall, puffing out his throat and staring back at her with unblinking eyes. Down on the beach there was the usual bird-life; dainty sandpipers waded in the shallow water and black cormorants rested on the rocky headlands, resting between fishing expeditions far out to sea.

'I'm bored,' Mia said with a loud sigh. 'What can I do?'

'Play the stone tower game,' Fleur suggested. 'See if you can beat your record of fifteen.'

So Mia scrabbled around to find a handful of small, flat stones then she began to balance them, one on top of the other. '… Six, seven, eight.'

'Careful,' Fleur warned as the tower wobbled.

'… Nine, ten, eleven.'

Just then there was a loud squeal from further up the mountain. A startled Mia jerked her hand and the tower of stones toppled.

'Huh!' She stood up and looked angrily up the slope.

Half a dozen macaque monkeys emerged from the forest and sprinted towards them. Two mothers carried babies on their backs, while the big male bared his teeth and led the group to Lookout Point, two hundred metres away from Mia and Fleur. They sat safely upwind of the family's high lookout fire, glancing back up the mountain towards the trees.

'Hmm, I wonder what scared them,' Fleur said,

glancing up towards the edge of the trees. She saw nothing unusual; only dry scrubland and rocks.

'The baby monkeys are so-o-o cute!' Mia left the waterfall and ventured a little way towards them. 'They've got big brown eyes and pointy pink ears. Fleur, come and look.'

Carrying the hatful of eggs with care, Fleur joined her sister on the slope. She loved the macaques even though they sometimes stole down to base camp at night and raided the Fishers' food store. They were a rich brown colour with funny dark tufts of hair on the top of their heads and they got into play-fights where they rolled on the ground and wrestled.

'Aah – one of the mothers is picking nits out of her baby's hair.' Mia crept closer.

'They're not nits, they're parasites.' Fleur smiled at the grooming ritual. Mia was right – the babies were cuter than cute. They were adorable.

'Same thing!'

'Well yes – I guess.' How much nearer could they creep without the macaques running off?

The male in the group watched every step they

made. It looked like he was playing a game of dare –
*OK, one more step and another and another, but
that's it; no more.* All of a sudden he opened his mouth
and let out a high-pitched screech. The whole group
leaped from the stone ledge and made a beeline straight
for the girls.

'Help, no – shoo, monkeys!' Mia squealed. She
grabbed Fleur's arm and dislodged the eggs inside
the hat.

'Whoa!' Fleur gave a cry. The eggs fell and smashed
on a rock.

In an instant the macaques forgot about the girls
and pounced on the broken eggs, scooping up the yolks
and cramming them into their mouths. Then they
licked their fingers and seemed to grin.

'Huh!' The danger over, Mia sulked and stamped
her foot.

'Yummy breakfast for monkeys,' Fleur grumbled.
Never mind – that was how life was sometimes on
Dolphin Island – frustrating and difficult. 'Come on,
Mia. We'll have to start looking all over again.'

*

'Where's Alfie?' James asked as he dished out scrambled eggs and fish fried in coconut oil for a late breakfast.

'He went to Turtle Beach to collect bamboo,' Fleur replied. It had taken ages to search a second time and gather enough eggs for the whole family. Now all she wanted to do was rest and eat.

'Mia, run and find him,' James suggested. 'Tell him I've made a feast fit for a king.'

Mia scooted off down the beach and disappeared over the headland.

'Here – we have to build up your strength.' James presented Fleur with fish and eggs on a plate salvaged from *Kestrel*. 'How are you feeling today?'

'Good,' she told him with her mouth full. 'I'd be even better if Jazz decided to pay me another visit.'

Her dad laughed. 'Yeah, yeah – but remember he has to live his own life and do what dolphins do.'

'Such as?' What could be more fun than swimming with her?

'Catching fish, hanging out with the rest of his pod – breaching, lob-tailing, riding the swell in front of ocean liners – cool stuff like that.'

'I guess.' Fleur wrinkled her nose and stared out to sea.

'You're not sulking, are you?' James checked. Four weeks on the island without shaving meant that his dark beard had grown bushy, his red T-shirt had faded in the sun and the hem on his only pair of shorts had begun to fray.

'No.'

'Not even a little bit?'

'No,' Fleur insisted. The longer she looked, the more certain she was that her dolphin friend was still nowhere to be seen. 'Oh well, I guess I'd better go and collect firewood for Lookout Point.'

'Good girl. Your mum's already up there. Tell her to come down for something to eat.'

As Fleur brushed herself down and got ready to leave camp, Mia reappeared with Alfie. They carried a big bundle of bamboo canes between them, pausing for a rest on the headland before trudging on.

'I'll let Mum know about the new load of bamboo. She'll probably want to get on with building the raft,'

Fleur said.

'You can bet your life she will,' James agreed.

So Fleur took the track up the cliff for the second time that day, picking her way from ledge to ledge until she came to Butterfly Falls. Here she stopped to cup her hands around her mouth and call up to her mum in her loudest voice. 'Mum – more bam-boo! And break-fast!'

Standing by the fire on Lookout Point, Katie heard her and gave her a thumbs-up. She immediately left the ledge and began her descent.

'Hey, Mum. Did you see any dolphins?' Fleur asked as their paths crossed.

'Hey, Fleury.' Katie greeted her daughter then shook her head. 'No. It's unusually quiet out there today, I must say.'

They paused to look out to sea, their hands shading their eyes against the bright sun. The empty horizon seemed to stretch for ever. There was a gentle swell as the white-capped waves met the underwater reef where *Merlin* had met her end.

'The tide's in,' Katie remarked. 'I might go down to

the water's edge in a little while to see if it's brought in anything useful, like old rope or empty bottles.'

'I'm collecting firewood,' Fleur explained. Even though there were no ships on the horizon or planes flying overhead, it was vital to keep both fires fed just in case.

So she said goodbye to her mum then walked on, searching under bushes for twigs and collecting an armful before she reached the lookout. She threw the fuel on the fire then went higher up the mountain in search of bigger branches that had fallen from the trees at the edge of the forest. But the trouble with Fleur was, she was easily thrown off-task. Not like Alfie, who set out to do a thing and saw it through to the end. Like fetching bamboo, for instance – he wouldn't stop hacking at the canes until he'd got enough to build a whole new raft. That was just the way he was. But as for Fleur collecting firewood – well, there were a dozen more interesting things to do.

There was investigating the termite mound at the far side of Lookout Point for a start. How fascinating it was to sit cross-legged on the hillside and watch the teeming columns of white ants go about their mysterious business, marching here and there, here and there. And what about the reddish-brown giant millipede she found attached to the first branch she collected? It was at least twenty centimetres long and deserved a full ten minutes of study. Then there was the crested chameleon sitting on a hot rock, staring at her with his bulbous eyes – not as pretty as George, her pet gecko, but interesting nonetheless.

Best of all, Fleur stood and watched a cloud of small white butterflies flit in the sunlight at the edge of the trees. So pretty. So dainty. She had to tear herself away from them and force herself to enter the shade of the forest, where suddenly the whole world changed.

Instead of light there was deep, dark shadow. If there were creatures in here, they weren't flitting anywhere. They were well hidden behind creepers, under logs or in the treetops. There were no birds singing.

Fleur let her eyes get used to the darkness then she crept forward along a fallen tree trunk, aiming to drag out a hefty branch that had broken off in a high wind. She hoped that this would provide enough wood to keep the fire going for a while. But she had to take care not to fall off the log into the muddy mess of creepers and decaying leaves beneath. That was how she'd picked up the tick that had made her so sick – by stepping into the mud and letting a tick attach itself to her ankle. There were other nasty things living here too. Poisonous snakes for all she knew. And there were definitely rats – she'd seen a big one the last time she was in here.

So she went slowly on all fours until she reached the fallen branch and found that it wasn't too heavy for her to drag it back the way she'd come.

It's Saturday. My friends back home are washing their hair and getting ready to go shopping, she thought ruefully as she heaved at the branch. *They're chatting about music and boys.*

Moving the branch roused a colony of bats in the trees overhead. They were pale creatures with thin, leathery wings that flitted deeper into the forest, away from danger.

It was a struggle, but at last Fleur dragged the dead branch out into the open and down the hillside to the fire. Once there, she wrenched at it and broke off short sections to feed the crackling flames.

'I'll go back into the forest for one more branch like that then I'll take a break,' Fleur said out loud, wiping sweat from her forehead. From her high vantage point she glanced down at the beach.

Alfie and her mum were busy laying out bamboo canes and cutting them all to the same length to build the raft. Mia and her dad played noughts and crosses on giant grids drawn in the sand.

Then Fleur took a long look out to the glittering sea. *Still no dolphins.* She gave a wistful sigh, then slowly and reluctantly made her way back up the mountain and into the forest.

Chapter Two

'OK, George – where are they?' After lunch Fleur sat with Mia on the beach at the entrance to George's Cave.

The cave was close to the shoreline and had been the very first place Fleur, Alfie and Mia had found to shelter in after *Merlin* had capsized and they'd been cast away on the uninhabited island. It was here that Fleur had befriended George the gecko.

'Where are who?' Mia wanted to know.

'Jazz, Stormy and Pearl, of course.' Fleur held out a tiny piece of jackfruit for George to nibble on then she raised her voice and called out in a loud voice: 'Come on, you three – you're supposed to be our best buddies. Where on earth have you got to?'

Little green George squatted on her bare shoulder, chewing contentedly.

Mia frowned and, standing hands on hips, mustered all the scorn of a know-it-all six-year-old. 'Why are you bothering to ask them? Dolphins can't talk, you know.'

'You want to bet?' Fleur said, grinning down at her. 'What do you think they're doing when they make all those whistles and clicking noises?'

'Yeah, but it's not actual words,' Mia insisted. She put one foot into the shallow water and hooked a piece of seaweed on to her toe. Waving her skinny leg in the air, she swung the dripping seaweed under Fleur's nose.

Cold water splashed against Fleur's hot cheeks and she shivered. 'It's as good as words.' With each hour that went by, she grew more impatient for a sighting of the dolphins. Yet again she shaded her eyes with her hands and stared out towards the horizon. Still no luck.

'OK,' she decided at last. 'Alfie's gone off to Turtle Beach again to collect bamboo. Let's go and lend a hand.'

So they paddled in shallow water at the water's edge towards the headland that separated Base Camp Bay from the neighbouring beach to the south. They'd almost reached the rocks when Alfie appeared on the headland, waving his arms and jumping up and down with excitement.

'Come quick!' he yelled.

Fleur and Mia began to run. They splashed through the water then scrambled up the rocks in time to see the sight that Fleur had been longing for.

There, in the shallows of the next bay were three sleek grey shapes. They swam just offshore, their curved dorsal fins cutting through the calm water, every so often raising their heads out of the water to shoot a jet of water out of the blowholes on the top of their domed heads.

'Yippee – there's Stormy!' Mia clapped her hands with delight before scrambling down the far side of the rocks. She'd recognized the black shading around his small, dark eyes. She dashed into the water at breakneck speed then swam out to greet him.

'I bet they've been looking for fish off Pirate Cave Beach,' Alfie said to Fleur. 'It's a good job I was having a rest from cutting canes. Otherwise I might have missed them.'

'So cool.' She gave a long, satisfied sigh. There was Jazz, doing his usual acrobatics. He leaped clear of the water, twisted in the air then slapped his tail flukes against the water as he landed. 'Show-off!' she laughed, kicking off her flip-flops before following Mia into the sea.

Alfie was determined not to be left behind. He took a different route – across the rocks to the very tip of the headland where he stood poised with his arms above his head, looking down into deep, clear water. He took a big breath, counted one-two-three then dived headlong. He entered the water cleanly with scarcely a splash then swam under the surface, only coming up for air when his lungs were ready to burst. Sploosh! He powered up from the depths and broke the surface, gasping for air. 'Hiya!' he said to Pearl, his very own dolphin pal.

She had a wide mouth that seemed to smile back at him. Her back was grey, her belly tinged with pearly pink. According to Alfie this made her by far the prettiest dolphin in the pod. And she was smaller than the other two – about a metre and a half long with an unusually curved fin that made her easy to single out.

Pearl swam close until they were eye to eye. She gave a series of birdlike chirps. *Hi to you too.*

Meanwhile Fleur said a special hello to Jazz. 'Hey, slow down,' she told him as he sped towards her. 'Yes, it's me. Where have you been?'

He swam in a rapid circle, making bubbles as he went. Fleur held her nose and ducked down under the surface to swim among the ring of sparkling bubbles. Then she came up and listened to Jazz's signature high-low, two-tone whistle – the happiest sound in the world. 'I love you too,' she told him as he stopped moving long enough for her to catch hold of one of his flippers and haul herself on to his back. Then they were off, straight out to sea, with Jazz cutting through the water and Fleur holding on to his fin for dear life.

'That's not fair – wait for me!' Mia saw Fleur climb astride Jazz and shoot off. In a flash she was on Stormy's broad back and they were following them, curving around the headland and heading towards Base Camp Bay. 'Race you!' she cried.

Alfie watched them speed away. He and Pearl took

their time. He grabbed her fin and swam alongside, enjoying the feeling of their bow wave splashing against his face. *What's the hurry?* he thought.

The sun was still high in the cloudless sky. There was no wind and no chance of a storm brewing up on the horizon. It was definitely a no-worries sort of day.

Slowly Pearl and Alfie rounded the headland to see Fleur and Mia playing a favourite game with Jazz and Stormy. The girls had slid off their backs into the water and were taking up position in front of their dolphins. They floated flat on their stomachs, bodies rigid, arms forward. The dolphins came up behind and pressed their beaks against the soles of Fleur and Mia's feet. Then whoosh! They set off at great speed, propelling the girls through the water ahead of them. Mia shrieked with delight. Fleur laughed out loud.

'Do it again!' Mia pleaded as soon as Stormy came to a halt. For her, this was better than any ride at Disney World.

Fleur let Jazz swim alongside her. 'Thanks for that – it was cool,' she murmured.

Lazy Pearl and Alfie were still lagging behind when

all at once Pearl opened her mouth and started to clap her jaws together. Then she gave off a series of short yelps. He'd never seen or heard this before and for a while it puzzled him. 'What's up?' he asked as he stroked the top of her head.

Again she clapped her jaws together. It was obviously a warning, but what about? Alfie looked ahead to make sure that Mia and Fleur were OK. He checked the beach and saw the campfire burning steadily as usual. There was no sign of their mum and dad. 'What is it?' he asked Pearl.

Whatever it was, she caught the attention of Jazz and Stormy who quickly rounded up Fleur and Mia and herded them towards the shore. Pearl did the same with Alfie, pushing him into the shallow water before she turned tail and swam back out to sea.

'What happened?' Fleur asked as she waded through shallow water until she reached Alfie.

'I'm not sure.' He couldn't work out what had brought the dolphin fun and games to a sudden end. Normally Pearl, Jazz and Stormy's visits lasted longer than this.

But there the young dolphins were, sticking close together, swimming out past the reef then turning and heading north about five hundred metres from the shore.

'Oh no!' It was Fleur who spotted what was wrong. She pointed straight out to sea, to a lone fin rising out of the water. The fin was larger than any dolphin's, and it wasn't curved, but straight.

Alfie and Mia recognized it straight away and their stomachs churned.

'Shark!' Alfie gasped.

The fin headed towards the shore. When it drew close to the reef, a sinister, wedge-shaped head appeared above the surface, followed by a long grey back topped by the triangular fin.

Fleur, Alfie and Mia were frozen to the spot. They knew that sharks could come in very close to the shore and put in amazing bursts of speed. Their teeth were razor-sharp.

The other thing they knew was that sharks were hunters. They ate anything they could find, including fish, seabirds, squid, turtles ... and young dolphins!

The shark came closer. They could make out dark stripes across its back. Past the reef it swam, through the turquoise water. It opened its wide jaws and displayed two rows of deadly, pointed teeth.

'Quick, come out of the water!' Fleur dragged Alfie and Mia on to the beach. 'Sharks can pick up vibrations when we move. That's how it knows we're here.'

'Will it eat us?' Mia cried. Her eyes were wide open and she struggled to draw breath.

'Not if we're on dry land.'

'Will it eat Stormy?' Mia wanted to know.

Fleur swallowed hard. She knew full well that the killer shark would go after Stormy, Jazz and Pearl the moment it realized they were nearby but she mustn't show Mia how worried she was. 'No,' she told her.

Mia didn't believe her. She began to cry.

Fleur tried again to soothe her. 'Don't worry, Mi-mi. Our dolphins are much too clever to get caught by an old tiger shark.'

Alfie frowned. He too kept quiet for Mia's sake. But he watched the shark in fear as it cruised the shallow waters of Base Camp Bay and he kept his fingers tightly

crossed behind his back, hoping and praying that it wouldn't pick up the vibrations that their dolphins had made as they swam out of reach.

Mia, Fleur and Alfie were so shaken by the appearance of the shark that they couldn't move. They stared at it and took in every detail.

'I reckon it's at least four metres long,' Alfie said in an awed voice.

'Look at its jaws.' Fleur shuddered. 'And its teeth!'

'It's nasty. I don't like it,' Mia wailed as she took hold of Alfie's hand.

They were too terrified to notice their dad come striding down the beach. He'd been snoozing inside the shelter but something had woken him up. He'd come out and straight away spotted the telltale fin. Shark alert! His one thought was to make sure that Alfie, Mia and Fleur stayed safe.

'Be very careful,' he said in a firm voice. 'The tide's still coming in. Stand well back.'

With her eyes fixed on the shark, Fleur held Mia's other hand and together they took a few steps backwards. They watched as the shark abruptly changed direction and cruised slowly between the two headlands.

'It's full-size but it's still a young one,' James said through gritted teeth. 'You can tell by the darkness of the stripes.'

The shark reached the headland between Base Camp Bay and Turtle Beach then suddenly, with a flick of its long, strong tail fin it changed direction again and swam swiftly across the bay in the direction that Pearl, Jazz and Stormy had taken. It reached the opposite headland and with another flick of its tail, disappeared from sight.

Mia grasped Alfie's and Fleur's hands even tighter. No one said a word.

Their dad was the first to break the silence. 'It's OK, he's gone. We're safe.'

Fleur just shook her head. Their dad didn't understand – it was the dolphins they were scared for, not themselves.

'But there'll be no swimming for a while,' James went on in a voice that was firmer and more serious than usual. 'It's not safe to go in the water while there are sharks around. You hear me, kids? No swimming until further notice.'

They turned to look at him, their eyes dark with fear. Meanwhile, their mum was hurrying down the cliff path, beckoning for them to come.

They ran up the beach to join her.

'Shark!' Mia gasped as her mum crouched down to put her arms around her.

'I know, Mi-mi. I was up at the lookout. I saw it.'

'Did you see where our dolphins went?' Fleur wanted to know. She held her breath and waited for the answer.

'I did,' Katie said. 'They were in a hurry so I reckon they knew the shark was there.'

Alfie nodded. 'Pearl definitely did. She was the one who signalled to Stormy and Jazz to warn them.'

'But did they get away?' Again, Fleur held her breath.

'Yes.' Katie's voice was calm. 'I watched it all from high up on the mountain. I saw the dolphins drop you off on our beach then I watched them swim off. You probably couldn't see them at that point but they definitely didn't hang around. They made straight out to sea.'

'Without the shark knowing which way they went?' Alfie checked.

'Hopefully,' Katie told him. 'They moved like lightning through the water. The last time I looked, the shark was still nosing around Echo Cave Beach and your lovely dolphins were clean out of sight.'

'Thank heavens!' Fleur gave a huge sigh of relief. It had been super-scary, but as long as Pearl, Jazz and Stormy were safely back with the rest of their pod, she could relax.

'That's enough excitement for one day,' James decided. 'How about we all go back to base camp and spend the rest of the afternoon building the raft?'

'Boring,' Mia exclaimed with a frown.

'But safe,' her mum said in the same calm voice. 'And useful. Come on, everyone, raft-building it is!'

Chapter Three

'Come to think of it, I suppose that's why it's been so quiet around here for the last day or two.' Fleur was still brooding over the appearance of the tiger shark next morning, when she and Alfie fetched fresh water from Butterfly Falls.

'Yes,' Alfie agreed. He filled a plastic bottle to the brim, listening to the slow glug-glug of the water as he gazed at the horizon. 'Dolphins know when there are sharks around. They use echolocation to pick up the signals. Sharks are pretty much the biggest things in the Torres Strait except for the odd whale or two. No way can dolphins miss them.'

'Thank goodness,' she added.

'Dad's serious about the no-swimming rule.' There was no top to the salvaged bottle so Alfie had to carry it carefully as he and Fleur set off down the cliff path. Her water container was a white plastic bag. She'd made a knot in the handles when it was full and now had to be careful to avoid the bushes on the way down. One prick from a sharp thorn and all the precious liquid would leak out.

'I know – it's really tough.' Swimming in the bay, even when Jazz wasn't around, was one of the most enjoyable things about living on Dolphin Island. It cooled you down for a start, and the feeling of floating on your back, looking up at the clear blue sky with the water buoying you up, was as close to heaven as it was possible to get. 'How long will the shark stick around, do you reckon?'

Ahead of her on the cliff path, Alfie shrugged. 'Who knows? You're the nature expert around here. You probably know more about them than I do.'

'I do know they don't stay in one place very long. I read about them online – before *Merlin* sank, obviously.' Their brilliant yacht had had every modern technological gadget on board, including the complicated navigation equipment that Alfie had loved. Her network system had been complete with an echo-sounder that could log your speed and map your course on a touch-screen plotter. And of course, she'd had the internet. 'Sharks are nomadic. They hunt alone, mostly at night and usually in warmer currents, close to the shore.'

Alfie half wished he hadn't asked. Fleur might be scatty about a lot of things, but when it came to facts about wildlife she had a photographic memory.

'They have pretty good eyesight.' She went on reciting word for word what she'd read. 'And an excellent sense of smell. They react to traces of blood in the water ... then they zoom in.'

'OK – that's enough,' Alfie muttered. If he hadn't been carrying the water bottle he would have blocked his ears with both hands.

'But like I said – they don't stick around for very long.'

'Good.' Alfie had reached the bottom of the cliff and began to push through the bushes to emerge on to the beach a few metres from their shelter. 'Don't tell Mia any of that – she's scared enough already.'

There was plenty more, but Fleur decided to keep it to herself. She knew, for instance, that sharks' teeth were so sharp they could slice through flesh and bone. They swam slowly and stealthily up to their prey then grabbed it and sometimes swallowed it whole. And there was nothing that a shark didn't see as food – she'd read about them trawling the seabed and gulping down rusty car number plates, strips of rubber, pieces of metal, plastic containers and all sorts of other rubbish.

Mia sat on a rock near the shelter, fanning herself with a palm leaf. 'I'm hot,' she complained as soon as she saw Alfie and Fleur.

'Go inside the shelter,' Alfie told her. 'It's nice and shady in there.'

'No. I want to go for a swim to cool down.'

'We're not allowed,' Fleur reminded her, taking the bottle of water from Alfie and letting Mia take a long swig. 'I'll tell you what, though. It's Sunday. That means it's the weekend. Why don't we have the afternoon off?'

'Good idea,' a voice from inside the shelter said and Katie emerged smiling brightly. 'Your dad's looking for firewood in Echo Cave. He and I can keep things going here for a while. You three should head off and have some fun.'

'Yay!' Mia grinned and jumped down from the rock. 'Where shall we go? What shall we do?'

'I've got an idea,' Alfie said. He for one would be glad to stop obsessing about sharks. 'You remember that old wreck I told you about?'

'The one in Black Crab Cove?' Fleur nodded and went into the shelter to find the map they'd made of Dolphin Island. It was drawn in charcoal on a piece of canvas they'd salvaged and it showed all the places they'd discovered so far. There was Echo Cave Beach to the north and Turtle Beach to the south. Below that there was Pirate Cave Beach and Black Crab Cove was to the south of that. Of the three kids, only Alfie had explored that far.

He pinpointed the cove with a stick. 'It's quite a long way,' he warned. 'What do you think, Mi-mi? Can you make it?'

'Yay!' she said again, jiggling about with excitement. 'Let's go.'

*

Alfie, Fleur and Mia were ready for their adventure. They'd put on some of their precious remaining sun cream and wore their hats low on their foreheads. Alfie brought a knife just in case they needed one to cut through shrubs and Fleur carried a big bottle of water in a makeshift backpack made from canvas and rope.

'Take care and make sure to be home before the sun goes down,' Katie told them. 'Don't split up whatever you do.'

They waved at her as they set off barefoot down the beach with Alfie leading the way. 'The wreck is really cool,' he promised. 'It's been there ages – since the olden days when they used to build ships out of wood.'

'Is it a pirate ship?' Mia asked.

'I dunno – could be.' He realized that it made things more exciting for Mia if she thought it was. Grinning at Fleur, he climbed up the first headland and felt cool spray from the waves settle on his face and arms. They crossed the rocks safely and jumped on to the sand of Turtle Beach. 'Ouch, it's hot!' he exclaimed. 'We'll have to walk in the water – it's cooler.'

'Stay right at the edge,' Fleur cautioned as the

memory of the tiger shark cruising the shoreline flashed back into her head.

They strode on without looking back to see their mum standing on the headland, watching their progress. Katie waited until they reached the edge of the neighbouring bay. *They look so small*, she thought. Her heart went out to them. *Small and brave*. Three barefoot kids in T-shirts and shorts, casting hardly any shadows in the midday sun. 'Stay safe,' she murmured as they disappeared from view.

*

Fleur, Alfie and Mia made steady progress across Pirate Cave Beach. The soft, wet sand slowed them down and the next headland seemed a long way off.

'Can we explore the cave?' Mia was keen to make a diversion. The last time she and Alfie had been here they'd crept into there to shelter from a storm and she'd had fun searching for hidden treasure. They'd had to crawl under an overhanging ledge and wriggle into the dark cavern, while outside rain and strong winds lashed the palm trees and sent waves crashing on to the shore.

Alfie shook his head. 'Not today – not if we want to get all the way to the wreck and back before dark.'

Mia looked pleadingly at Fleur.

'Alfie's the boss,' Fleur told her.

Alfie forged ahead. 'Avast, mi hearties! I'm the captain of this ship. You two have to follow my orders. Quick march!'

His pirate drawl made Mia laugh. She swung her arms and marched smartly on.

'Who knows if there be gold on the wreck?' Bringing up the rear, Fleur copied Alfie's pirate voice. 'Gold and silver, diamonds and pearls, aaargh!'

The game of make-believe made time pass more quickly and soon they reached the rocks where they found hundreds of tiny, dark crabs in the rock pools. A white heron was fishing for anchovies in one of the shallow pools but flapped away as soon as they arrived.

Alfie, Mia and Fleur scrambled over the headland as fast as they could. The rocks were sharp underfoot and they were afraid the crabs might nip their toes. They jumped down into the next wide bay and looked up the dazzling white beach.

At first Mia and Fleur made out only palm trees and thick, tangled bushes fringing the sand. The beach was smooth and undisturbed.

'Where's the wreck?' Mia asked impatiently.

Alfie pointed. 'There – beside the big rock.'

Eventually Fleur and Mia spotted the upturned wooden hull, bleached by the sun and half hidden by sand dunes. It was about thirty metres long and tilted steeply towards its port side. The moment she saw it, Mia began to sprint up the beach.

Fleur and Alfie followed. 'Ouch – ouch – ouch!' Fleur muttered as the hot sand scorched the soles of her feet. She had to run fast to reach the shade of the trees where she sat on a rock, raised her feet and breathed a sigh of relief.

'What do you think?' Alfie asked as they stared at the remains of an old sailing ship.

'It's huge!' Fleur whispered. She stared up at decayed planks still coated with ancient barnacles and the remains of three tall masts lying splintered on the rocks. There was a row of round portholes along the side and a rotten figurehead – the head and bust of a woman with long hair. Her eyes, nose and mouth were almost worn away by the weather. 'And really old.'

'Hundreds of years,' Alfie agreed. 'But look – you can still see the ship's name.'

Fleur tried to read the letters carved into the wood. Slowly she made out a 'D' and an 'O'.

Alfie stepped in to help her. '*Dolphin*. She's called *Dolphin*. How cool is that?'

'Cool!' Mia clapped her hands. Scenting pirate treasure, she started to look for a way to get inside the hull and soon found a gap between broken boards. Without a second thought she squeezed through and before Alfie and Fleur knew it, she was gone.

'Whoo-oo!' Mia's hollow voice echoed from inside the wreck. 'It's spooky in here. Yuck – cobwebs!'

'Any treasure?' Fleur winked at Alfie then followed her in. As her eyes grew used to the shadows, she saw that sand had drifted inside the hull and covered everything in a thick layer that was soft, silky and cool to the touch. Long, dry grass grew in crevices – an ideal home for crickets, spiders and insects of all kinds.

Alfie was the last to lower himself into the belly of

the ship to explore. He poked around in dark corners until he felt something square and brushed away layers of sand to expose a large wooden chest underneath a broken bench.

'Yay – what's that?' Mia held her breath as she watched him lift the lid.

The rusty hinges creaked then up popped the head of a small yellow lizard with staring eyes. When it saw the intruders, it leaped out of the chest and scuttled off.

'That made me jump,' Alfie muttered. Gingerly, he felt inside the chest and touched a smooth, round object which he lifted out with great care. It had a handle and a spout and was made of brown clay. There was a big crack from top to bottom.

'It's a boring old jug.' Expecting gold and silver, Mia's face fell. 'What else is there?'

He drew out a plate made of dull grey metal, then a second and a third.

'Cool – they'll come in useful. We'll take them back with us.' Fleur took the heavy plates and managed to hide her own disappointment. It felt weird to be inside the wreck, coming across everyday objects that the crew of *Dolphin* had used all those years ago. 'I can't help wondering what happened to the men,' she murmured. She tried hard to push away thoughts of the ghosts of sailors haunting the spot where their ship had gone down.

Alfie stuck with practical things. 'Three plates and a jug – that's all there is in here,' he said as he put aside the broken jug then lowered the lid. 'This chest could be useful too,' he decided. 'As long as it's not too heavy to lift.'

'Where's the treasure?' Mia wondered as she kept on searching. 'Pirates always have treasure.'

'Maybe these weren't pirates, Mi-mi.' Fleur had scared herself by thinking about ghosts and she was ready to leave. 'They were probably ordinary sailors who got caught in a storm, poor things.'

'Maybe fishermen,' Alfie suggested. 'Perhaps they had a lifeboat and they got into it and rowed away before their ship capsized.'

'I don't know about you two, but I need a breath of fresh air.' Fleur squeezed back out through the gap, glad to feel the sun on her face once more. She put the plates on the sand then scrambled up the outside of the hull towards the tilting deck. Here she discovered a coil of thick rope and the tattered remains of a canvas sail. 'Come and look at this,' she called to the others.

Alfie and Mia emerged into the sunlight to see Fleur lugging a coil of heavy rope across the sloping deck.

'Stand clear. I'm going to throw it down to you,' she warned. She lifted the rope then gave a sudden, sharp cry as she dropped it again and backed off as far as she could.

'What's up?' Alfie yelled.

'Snake!' she muttered.

The creature had hidden itself inside the coil of rope. It was bright green – a long, thin, scaly snake that raised its flat head and flicked its forked tongue towards her.

'What kind?' Alfie kept tight hold of Mia's hand.

'Viper,' Fleur said through gritted teeth. Deadly poisonous. One strike and she would be in serious trouble. She was glued to the spot, hardly daring to breathe.

Alfie felt a tight knot form in his stomach. But if

anyone knew what to do it would be Fleur.

The snake's head swayed. It shot its tongue towards her. For what felt like an age it kept her in its sights.

If Fleur moved a muscle, it might spell disaster. *Stay still. Stay still.*

The viper swayed from side to side. Then, to her massive relief, it uncoiled along its length and started to slither slowly across the deck, away from Fleur towards the starboard edge of the deck.

Alfie and Mia saw its head appear. They too stood stock-still as it eased from the deck over the side and through the nearest porthole.

Alfie waited until the tip of the snake's tail had disappeared. 'OK, it's gone inside the hull,' he reported to Fleur, who took a deep breath and looked for the quickest way down, grabbing the figurehead to swing herself over the prow then jump down on to the beach. Mia ran to her and threw her arms around her waist.

'I'm OK,' Fleur told them, smiling and trying to laugh it off even though her legs were still shaking. 'But no way am I going back in there for that wooden chest.'

'Me neither,' Mia and Alfie chorused.

Without saying another word, they collected the three plates and set off down the beach. They stopped at the shoreline and looked back at the wreck. All was quiet. Waves rippled and foamed around their ankles. The white heron that they'd disturbed earlier had perched on the ship's figurehead and was watching them go.

'That was close,' Alfie murmured. He shuddered to think how quickly a sunny adventure could turn into deadly danger here on Dolphin Island. 'You're sure you're OK?' he checked with Fleur.

'I'm fine,' she answered. 'Everything's cool. Are you hungry, Mi-mi?'

'Starving,' Mia said, breaking free and splashing ahead through the shallow waves towards the rocks. 'Race you both. The last one home has to collect firewood!'

Chapter Four

Night times on the island were often bad for Alfie. He had nightmares about *Merlin* being shipwrecked on the reef and he would feel himself falling from the deck into stormy water, crying out for help all over again. Then he would wake up with a start and spend hours lying in the dark with his eyes open, listening to mysterious noises outside the shelter.

It happened that night, after they'd got back from visiting the wreck.

In his uneasy sleep he heard the wind roar and felt the waves lift the boat into the air then plunge it back down into the dark depths. He was on deck, clinging to the guardrail, losing his footing, being tossed overboard.

He jerked awake and sat up with his whole body shaking.

'Alfie?' Fleur murmured. Like him, her sleep had been broken by bad dreams. 'Are you awake?'

'Yep.' They kept their voices low so as not to disturb the others. The door to the shelter was covered by a worse-for-wear insect screen that had washed up on the shore, through which Fleur and Alfie could see the glow of the campfire.

'Do you want to go outside and talk?'

'OK.' While Fleur silently shifted the screen to one side, he rolled off his sleeping platform and followed her out. 'I had a bad dream,' he confessed.

'Me too. Mine was about being bitten by a poisonous snake. It gave me a bad fever all over again. How about you?'

'It was about *Merlin* sinking.' Alfie was glad of the cool breeze.

Fleur fetched dry wood from the stack and threw it on the fire. The wood crackled and orange sparks flew upwards into the darkness. 'Just think – if we could text people at school and tell them we'd been cast away on a tropical island, everyone would say it was so cool.' She sighed wistfully. 'They'd think it was paradise. And it is, some of the time.'

'But not all,' Alfie pointed out. Kids back home didn't know about the howling storms that ripped through the palm trees, or about snakes and sharks and dark, dark forests that you were scared to enter. They wouldn't understand about the nightmares.

Fleur looked up at a bright moon. Silvery clouds scudded across the starlit sky. 'Fancy a walk?' she asked Alfie.

He nodded and they strolled in silence down to the water's edge, feeling sand between their toes and hearing nothing but the waves breaking against the rocks.

'This is Day 29,' he reminded her once they'd stopped ankle-deep in the water. 'I've been counting it up – did you know we've been *almost* rescued five times?'

'Almost,' she echoed, her voice still sad.

'Number one – a plane flew overhead on Day 3.'

'But it was too high to see our *Help* sign written in the sand.'

'Number two – on Day 6 we saw a ship.'

'Ditto – too far away.'

'Then it was ages before we got another chance. Day 17 – there was a container ship on the horizon. That was number three. Pearl and the others did their best to attract the sailors' attention.'

'Even they couldn't make it turn towards our tiny island.' Fleur remembered each of these occasions all too well.

'Number four – those two yachtsmen in *Kestrel* got blown off-course in a storm. We thought they might see the smoke from our fires but they were too busy scrambling into the lifeboat before their boat sank.'

'That was seven days ago. Two days later, another plane flew overhead.' Hopes had risen but were soon dashed. This incident had ended in bitter disappointment like all the rest.

'Yep – number five.' Alfie stood and stared out to sea. 'Fleur, does it make you think ...'

'What?' she prompted irritably. Somehow at night, under the moon and stars, she felt more completely lost than ever. Here they were: two lonely castaways on a tiny island in a vast, dark universe.

'That we'll never be rescued,' he said in a low, quiet voice.

'Don't say that,' she pleaded. Her eagle eyes had spotted movement on the horizon but she waited a while before she said anything to Alfie. 'I know it's not easy but we just have to be patient, that's all. And think of the good things about being here.'

'Like what?' Alfie's nightmare had made him extra gloomy.

Her answer came quickly and she pointed straight ahead. 'Dolphins for a start.'

He snapped out of his bad mood and was suddenly alert. 'Where?'

'Right there, about fifty metres out, swimming this way.'

It was true – their three dolphins approached swiftly, clearly visible in the moonlight. Water glistened on their backs as they rose to the surface to give out their

signature whistles: high-low from Jazz, a shrill monotone from Stormy and Pearl's very own birdlike chirrup.

Alfie gave a small whoop of delight. He ran knee-deep into the waves and was about to plunge right in when Fleur caught up with him and held him back.

'No swimming – remember. We can't go in the water because of the shark.'

He pulled himself free. 'But our dolphins would know if the shark was anywhere near.'

Pearl, Jazz and Stormy seemed perfectly happy. They frolicked in the waves, turning belly-up to scud with their flippers in a lazy backstroke or else doing a complete roll before vanishing out of sight.

'I know – and I'm dying to go in too,' Fleur admitted. She watched Jazz do his favourite trick of rising up on to his tail flukes and dancing on the surface. She waved at him with both hands. 'What do you think, Alfie – do we dare?'

'I'm not sure.' Now he was the one to pull back from the brink of breaking their dad's latest rule.

Sorely tempted to take a midnight dip, Fleur and Alfie were startled by more dolphins surging past the reef towards the shore.

'It's the whole pod,' Alfie realized when he saw an adult male almost three metres long and soon after that Pearl's mother, Marina. She broke away from the group and darted through the water towards her calf.

The amazing sight of a dozen dolphins churning up the water at the edge of the bay kept Alfie and Fleur rooted to the spot. They watched Marina speed through the waves until she reached Pearl. Then she did something they'd never seen before. Raising her powerful tail out of the water, she gave Pearl a solid whack with her flukes.

'Ouch!' Alfie gasped.

Marina did it a second time then began to nudge Pearl away from the shoreline, back out towards the reef. At the same time other fully grown adults approached Jazz and Stormy and hustled them out of the bay.

'Look at that. The grown-ups are telling them off for paying us a visit,' Fleur realized. Though she was sorry to see them go, she couldn't help smiling at the thought of Jazz, Pearl and Stormy acting like badly behaved teenagers.

Alfie didn't smile. 'I guess that means the tiger shark is still around.' Why else would Marina and the others show up if it wasn't to make sure that the whole pod stuck together? There was safety in numbers, after all.

'I guess it does,' Fleur said with a sigh. She scanned the bay for the shark's telltale triangular fin and felt a shiver through her when she spotted a dark, pointed shape among the white waves breaking on the reef.

'Look, Alfie – over there!' she gasped.

He followed her pointing finger. 'Don't worry, it's only a rock,' he decided, as the waves frothed and the shape disappeared.

The panic was over for now. They stood at the shore for a long time to drink in the sight of the dolphin pod speeding away, breaching the waves and blowing water out of their blowholes, twisting and turning as they went.

*

As the sun rose and Mia, Katie and James woke, the castaways went about their daily routine of collecting water and building up their fires. They had breakfast of fish and jackfruit, washed down with coconut milk.

After breakfast, Fleur checked their food store which was kept in a gap between two rocks under a canvas cover. The store was close to the entrance to their shelter. 'We need more jackfruit,' she reported. 'I can fetch some after I've stoked up the lookout fire.'

'Nice one, Fleury,' her dad said. He and Alfie had planned a fishing expedition off the southern headland, hoping to bring back a decent-sized snapper for dinner. Katie and Mia meanwhile wanted to stay at base camp to carry on working on the raft.

So Fleur climbed the cliff path alone. She was perfectly happy to take her time and do more nature study, all the while keeping a close watch for activity out to sea.

'Neat,' she said when she saw a bush turkey break cover from under a thorn bush close to the path. Then, 'Cute!' when a pair of geckos allowed her to approach close enough to inspect their enormous, lidless eyes and even the little suction pads on the underside of their splayed toes. *George will be pleased when I fetch more jackfruit*, she thought as she started the task of collecting firewood.

When she reached the lookout ledge, she could see that the fire was low and would need building up. 'I guess that means going into the forest again,' she grumbled to herself. 'Never mind – I can collect fruit at the same time.'

She carried on up the mountain until she came to a tall jackfruit tree. Some of the football-sized fruit lay on the ground under the tree but these were too bruised and mushy for eating so she peered up into the branches. There must be one or two ripe ones up there ready to fall. All she had to do was fetch a long stick and knock one free, standing ready to catch it when it plummeted down. She was still looking for the juiciest fruit and thinking of all the things you could do with it – eat it fresh, cut it into strips and dry it in the sun, mush it into a puree, roast the seeds in the fire – when a monkey parted the spear-shaped leaves and peered down at her. He tilted his head to one side and showed her the chunk of jackfruit he held in his hand – yellow and juicy and just right to eat.

'It looks like you beat me to it,' Fleur said with a grin.

The macaque quickly disappeared behind the leaves while Fleur searched for a stick long enough to reach the lower branches. She found one a few metres away then went back to the tree.

'OK,' she said to herself. 'Watch out, monkey – wherever you are.' She raised the sturdy stick and aimed it at a bulbous fruit that looked just right.

Her idea worked. She knocked the end of the stick against the chosen fruit. It came free and she caught it in both hands. Success!

Fleur was pleased with herself. Ready to try again, she placed it on the ground then raised the stick a second time.

But a nearby kerfuffle distracted her. It came from inside the forest – the sound of a creature crashing through the undergrowth. No, it was more than one, Fleur decided. She heard twigs breaking, leaves rustling, feet running. It was at ground level, not up in the trees. So it wasn't monkeys or tree kangaroos. What was it then? Fleur lowered the stick and, wielding it as a weapon at the ready, waited for the creatures to emerge.

Something let out a snort then a loud, high squeal.

Fleur held her ground. There was another squeal. Then a bulky animal burst out of the shadows into the sunlight. It was dark brown and had pointed tusks and a broad snout.

Fleur held her breath, hardly able to believe her eyes. There was a wild boar here on Dolphin Island. This was amazing – something that they'd never suspected before now. More than one, she confirmed as a second boar broke cover of the forest and hurtled down the steep, rocky slope, immediately followed by four babies. Wild-eyed and breathless, the family scattered across the hillside.

Fleur's senses were on full alert. She saw their terror, heard the heavy, slow thud of feet following the boars through the forest undergrowth. The footsteps suddenly halted, leaves rustled. There was a long hiss and then silence.

Panic rose into Fleur's throat. This was no ordinary jungle predator. This was something enormous that made even wild boars take flight. Still holding the stick in front of her like a spear, she began her retreat.

She stepped backwards away from the dark

shadows. There was another hiss and a rustle of leaves. Further down the slope, the boars gathered – the male and female, with their four little ones. They regrouped then set off back the way they'd come, but cautiously skirting the edge of the forest until they disappeared over the brow of the hill.

If wild boars ran from the unknown threat, no way was Fleur prepared to stick around. She tried not to make any sound as she backed off towards Lookout Point. But the ground was stony and her feet dislodged loose gravel that rattled down the hill. Fleur panicked again. She dropped the stick, turned and ran all the way to Butterfly Falls where she paused to draw breath. She looked up towards the top of the mountain. Was anything following her? No, the coast was clear. But her heart was pounding and her mouth was dry with fear.

Quickly she scrambled down the cliff path on to the beach, calling for her mum.

'What is it?' Katie stopped lashing together lengths of bamboo with twine. 'You look as if you've seen a ghost.'

'Where's the jackfruit?' Mia wanted to know. She stood with her toy monkey tucked under one arm.

Fleur reached the shelter and drew a deep breath. 'I left it behind. Guess what – there's a family of wild boars living in the forest.'

'Blimey.' Katie was nonplussed. This was news, certainly, but it didn't explain why Fleur seemed so scared.

'Seriously, there is – I saw them when I was collecting the fruit.'

'Hmm – that must have been quite a surprise.'

'Yes. Two adults and four babies. I have no idea how they got here.' Fleur knew that boars weren't usually found on these islands.

'The same way goats got on to that small island we visited off the coast of Queensland,' Katie guessed. 'The boars were probably dropped off by sailors following the spice routes, or else they swam here themselves.'

'The thing is ...' Fleur took another breath, '... they were running away.'

Mia hugged her soft toy, Monkey, closer to her chest. 'What from?'

'That's just it – I don't know!' Fleur's eyes were wide as she explained what had just happened. She told them about the macaque eating the jackfruit, about her search for the long stick and the sounds that came from the forest. 'Trampling noises, then grunts and squeals. And after that there was something slow and heavy and then a long, horrible hiss.'

'Was it a snake?' Mia remembered the scary green viper in the *Dolphin* wreck.

Fleur shook her head. 'No, I heard footsteps.'

'Whatever it was, I'm glad you didn't hang around to find out.' Katie was always on the side of being sensible and staying safe. She reminded Fleur of one of the island rules that they'd made soon after they'd arrived. 'No going deep into the forest alone, remember.'

'And no sailing off by yourself like Alfie did,' Mia reminded her. 'We all have to stick together.'

'Even more so now that we know that something dangerous may be living in the forest,' their mum said firmly.

No swimming with dolphins. No sailing. No going into the forest. Fleur frowned. The list of rules was growing longer day by day.

Chapter Five

'One for all!' Alfie took the lead up the cliff path. He set up a chant that Fleur and Mia finished off with cheery voices.

'All for one!'

'One for all – all for one!' they chorused again.

They'd waited in the shade of the palm trees behind base camp for the sun to pass its height and now they were climbing the cliff to bring back the jackfruit that Fleur had left lying on the ground earlier that morning.

'Wait a minute – that's the wrong way round. Isn't it supposed to be "All for one – one for all!"?' she queried.

'Who cares? We're the Three Musketeers in any case.' Alfie strode ahead.

'Who are they? Are they pirates?' Mia asked. She'd added more feathers to her hat and wore a shell necklace that hung down to her waist, over a long Cinderella T-shirt that Alfie had salvaged after *Merlin* went down.

'Kind of,' Fleur replied. 'They were French.'

'French pirates!' Mia grinned with satisfaction. 'Avast, mi hearties!'

'Yo-ho-ho and a bottle of rum!' Alfie was determined not to think too much about sharks or creatures that lurked in the forest. He decided to concentrate on food instead. 'Hey, did you know that Dad and I caught a ginormous snapper?' Stopping by the waterfall, he held his hands wide apart. 'It's this big. We're going to grill it over the fire for supper tonight.'

The delicious thought made their stomachs rumble. 'With jackfruit for pudding,' Fleur promised. She smiled even though she felt nervous about returning to the fruit tree at the edge of the forest.

'Mi-mi, do you want a drink?' Alfie offered her the water bottle that he'd brought with him.

Doing her best to control her nerves, Fleur was the first to set off again. She was doing fine until they came within twenty metres of the tree. 'Uh-oh,' she said, pointing towards scuffed footprints in a patch of fine gravel. 'Does that look like trotter marks to you?'

'Boar tracks.' Alfie nodded his agreement. 'Lots of them.' He followed the curving trail down the mountainside.

'See, I wasn't making it up,' Fleur muttered. All pretence of keeping calm had melted away and now all she wanted to do was to grab the fruit and hurry back to camp.

'There's our jackfruit.' Mia spotted the leathery golden fruit lying beneath the tree and ran ahead. 'It's heavy,' she cried as she picked it up then stubbed her toe on something pointed. 'Ouch!'

Alfie stooped to pick up the object. It was smooth and curved and it didn't take him long to work out that it was a bone from an animal's ribcage, stripped clean by the rain and bleached white by the sun. When he looked more closely at the ground, he found more ribs, two leg bones and a skull nearby.

Fleur and Mia joined him to inspect his find. They noticed that the skull had two rows of sharp teeth and a pair of curved tusks.

'Yuck, what's that?' Mia shrank back in disgust.

'It's a boar's skull,' he told her as he glanced across at Fleur.

Mia wrinkled her nose. 'It's dead, poor thing.'

'Yes, it's definitely dead,' Alfie agreed.

It was probably killed by the creature I heard. Fleur managed to keep this frightening thought to herself and was surprised when Alfie picked up the leg bones and put them into his shorts pocket. 'What are you planning to do with them?'

'I'm not sure yet.'

'So why bring them with us?'

'Because they could be useful, that's why.'

'How can old bones be useful?' Fleur didn't get it. Like Mia, she thought the remains of the dead boar were nasty, especially when she imagined how the poor animal had most likely met its end as supper for the mystery hunter.

'I dunno. I'm bringing them just in case.'

Fleur recognized her brother's stubborn look. Not wanting to hang around longer than she had to, she took the big jackfruit from Mia and together they followed him down the hill. No one was in the mood for talking. Instead, they kept their eyes peeled for a sighting of Jazz, Stormy and Pearl, and when they arrived at camp they split off and did their own thing.

Mia went into the shelter to make a necklace out of miniature shells. 'It's for Monkey,' she told her dad, who was raising the sleeping platforms higher off the ground by stacking up flat stones at each corner.

'Lucky Monkey,' James said with a grin. The idea behind altering the beds was to raise them clear of creepy-crawlies that crept under the screen at night. 'What are your brother and sister up to?'

'Fleur went down to George's Cave to feed him.'

'Feed him what?'

'Jackfruit. He thinks it's yummy. Alfie's got some bones.'

'Hmm.' Curious, James went outside to take a look. He found Alfie perched on a rock close to the food store. His son's hair caught the light and shone the colour of pale honey. 'Hey – what's up?'

Alfie held up one of the bones. 'I want to make a knife.'

His dad sat down beside him. 'How?'

'I reckon I could whittle this bone into shape with one of our steel knives.'

James considered the idea then nodded. 'OK. It might take a while though.'

'I don't care. Anyway, it's something to do.'

'When you're not helping to build the raft or looking for firewood or fishing or manning the lookout …' James ran through the jobs that kept them busy all day long.

'Can I though?'

James looked at him long and hard then nodded and leaned over to pat Alfie's knee. 'Whittle away, son. Make whatever you like.'

*

Mia loved the job of marking the calendar stick. Most mornings she woke early and carved the next notch. Day 30. Day 31. Day 32. Nothing but sun and blue sky. No wind. No clouds.

The hours between dawn and dusk were filled with the usual tasks and the only difference was that Alfie used his spare time to carve and whittle at the bones they'd found.

'Have you seen Alfie's knife?' Mia asked Fleur as

they sat outside George's Cave to watch the sun go down. She dug a hole in the wet sand, stood in it then waited for the shallow waves to swirl in and fill it.

'Not lately.' Life had been so quiet these last few days that Fleur almost wished they could have a storm. At least bad weather would liven things up. 'Why?'

'He's making a handle out of bamboo. Shall we go and see?'

'If you like.' Stopping to check that George was settled for the night on his favourite ledge inside his cave, Fleur followed Mia up the beach. They found Alfie on the rock next to the food store, head bowed and hands busy.

'Hi, Alfie. Show Fleur your knife.' Non-stop Mia scrambled up the rock to sit next to him.

'It's not finished yet,' he muttered. He was happy with the way the bone blade had turned out but he was still working on the handle.

'Show her anyway.'

So Alfie handed over his unfinished masterpiece.

'Wow!' Fleur was impressed. The edges were sharp and the blade came to a deadly point. He'd lashed the

70

handle to the blade with thin twine. 'That's cool, Alfie.'

'What are you going to use it for?' Mia asked.

'I dunno yet. Loads of things. It'll cut up jackfruit and yams, yucca roots and palm leaves – stuff like that.'

'It's really, really cool. Will you make one for me?' an excited Mia wanted to know.

By now the sun had sunk and left them in semi-darkness. James and Katie were making their way down from Lookout Point where they'd stoked up the fire for the night.

As the shadows lengthened and deepened, Fleur, Alfie and Mia continued to talk about making more knives. They failed to notice movement in the bushes behind the shelter. A monkey emerged and made its stealthy way towards the food store where it pulled at the canvas covering with nimble fingers.

'I could make a knife for you too, if you like,' Alfie said to Fleur after he'd given way to Mia's pleading. He'd found the bone tricky to whittle down at first, but he knew that practice would make perfect.

The monkey twitched his tail then tugged harder at

the covering. He dislodged a stone that was keeping the canvas weighted down. The stone fell with a light thud on to the sand.

Fleur glanced across to see what had made the noise. 'Hey!' she cried.

The macaque kept on tugging. He dislodged more stones to reveal the stored coconuts, yucca roots and

dried fish. The second he saw the food he made a grab for the nearest coconut.

'Hey!' Mia and Alfie joined in with Fleur.

'Quit that – shoo!' Fleur yelled. She was first down from the rock, ready to tackle the cheeky intruder.

But he wasn't about to be caught. Realizing that he'd been spotted, he screeched then raised the

coconut above his head and threw it at Fleur. She ducked. The missile hit the rock and cracked open.

'Shoo!' Mia shouted and waved her arms. 'Naughty!'

'That food doesn't belong to you!' Alfie lunged at the macaque.

So the monkey took flight. He scampered down the beach past Mia, Fleur and Alfie and was soon joined by three others. They shot out of the bushes, their faces lit by the glare of the campfire flames. Chattering madly, they brushed past the kids and followed their leader towards the shore.

Fleur, Alfie and Mia gave chase but they were no match for the macaques, who climbed on to the nearest headland and did a crazy dance in the dying light. They jumped up and down and leaped from rock to rock, splashing through pools before tumbling down the far side into Echo Cave Beach.

'Phew!' Fleur watched them leave. 'That was close.' The monkeys' latest raid made her realize they would have to improve their food store security.

'They're funny,' Mia giggled.

'Not so funny when you think they could have

stolen all our food,' Alfie pointed out.

They stood a while and kept watch in case the monkeys crept back. Waves lapped the shore. The moon appeared low in the sky.

Quietly at first, just loud enough to hear above the gently breaking waves, they heard familiar whistles coming from far out to sea. There was no mistaking them – three different sounds signalling the return of Pearl, Jazz and Stormy.

'Did you hear that?' Fleur turned towards the sea and spread her arms wide ready to welcome them.

The dolphins swam towards the shore, sure and steady. There was no sign of the rest of the pod – just the three youngsters paying a peaceful moonlit visit.

Alfie gave a beaming smile. 'This way!' he yelled. 'We're over here!'

Mia danced along the shoreline, too happy to say anything.

And so the three dolphins whistled and swam into the bay, leaping clear of the water and twisting and turning in the air. Their torpedo bodies glistened and gleamed as they approached the beach.

'Do you realize what this means?' Fleur swept Mia off her feet and swung her round until she was dizzy. 'Marina and the other adults don't need to keep an eye on them any more. The shark has moved on.'

With her feet back on firm ground, Mia laughed and clapped her hands. 'For ever and ever?'

'Maybe – we can't say for sure.' Alfie ran waist-deep into the water. He reached out to stroke the top of Pearl's head. She swam closer still and nudged him with her beak. 'All we know is that he's not here now.'

Mia darted into the waves. She threw her arms around Stormy. 'I missed you so much!' she cried as he blew out through his blowhole and sent a jet of water showering over her.

Sweet-natured Jazz loved his cuddles and kisses. He swam close to Fleur and scudded with his flippers to stay in one place. The dark shading around his eyes showed up clearly in the moonlight.

'Hey,' she said softly. She ventured out into the water until her feet could no longer touch the bottom then she started to swim. Jazz clicked and slowly circled around her before he came close enough for her to put an arm around him. They swam together in a wider circle, moving slowly through the gentle swell of the waves. Fleur enjoyed every second. 'Hey, Jazz – am I glad to see you,' she murmured.

Chapter Six

The storm that Fleur had wished for during an idle moment came the following day. It was sudden and fierce, blowing in from the east without warning and catching the family by surprise.

Alfie and Mia were gathering firewood on Echo Cave Beach when the storm hit. It began with a high wind that tore through the palm trees behind the cave and whipped up a sandstorm that forced them to take shelter.

'Quick – in here!' Alfie made Mia cover her eyes as he dragged her into the cave before the rain started.

From here they watched the waves rise and break over the rocks. Spray was flung high into the air. Soon a thick mist swirled up the beach, cutting visibility and deadening the thud and crash of the waves.

Seconds later, rain lashed down on to the beach,

falling fast and furious and making Mia and Alfie even more glad of their shelter.

'I hope the others aren't getting too wet,' Alfie muttered. While the storm raged, he told Mia they had to sit as far back from the cave entrance as they could.

'Me too.' Mia hugged her knees to her chest and tried not to worry about her mum and dad, Fleur, George and Monkey.

*

Over in Base Camp Bay Fleur had abandoned her morning task of reorganizing the family's food store and taken refuge in the shelter. *I'd better be careful what I wish for in future*, she decided as she stared out through the doorway. Luckily, another refugee from the storm had beaten her to it. George had already fled inside. He clung to the shelter wall, listening to the raindrops splash down on to the palm leaf roof. 'I know, George,' she said with a miserable sigh as she checked for leaks. 'This is a pretty bad storm. It means that Jazz, Stormy and Pearl will be miles out to sea. They'll be deep underwater, staying safe until it's all over.'

The gecko spotted a juicy black spider keeping dry by clinging to the calendar stick. He flicked out his long lizard tongue, grabbed it and gobbled it up.

 'Anyway, thank goodness we're out of it,' Fleur muttered.

Outside, the wind howled through the trees and the rain threatened to douse the campfire flames.

Fleur spotted the danger just in time. Braving the storm, she dashed out and fed the fire with dry driftwood. It hissed and spat. The flames flickered. 'Come on, fire,' Fleur urged. 'Don't go out on me, please!'

Fire was at the heart of everything here on Dolphin Island. The Fishers relied on it for keeping warm during the cold nights and for cooking the fish they caught. Most important of all, they needed it for signalling to any passing ship or plane.

The torrential rain went on and on. Fleur realized she needed to do more to protect the flames and she had to act fast. So, braving the full force of the wind and rain, she struggled to reach the woodpile stacked against the cliff. She pulled out four long sticks, the straightest and strongest she could find. She rammed the ends into the sand to form a square of upright poles around the fire. Again she fought against the wind to reach the food store and drag the heavy canvas cover from its niche in the rock. Finally she slung this over the pole frame then lashed it and tied it down securely with rope to make a temporary roof for the fire.

Fleur prayed that it would work. 'Please don't blow away,' she muttered as she retreated into the shelter. She drew breath and watched as the fresh driftwood at last caught fire. Dense blue smoke billowed out from under the canvas. It blew into the shelter, caught in her throat and made her cough. But her plan seemed to be working – new flames slowly flickered into life.

Relieved, Fleur kept a careful watch. If the flames grew too strong and leaped up towards the canvas, she would have to dash outside again to save it from catching light. It was touch and go – right now the fire was well ablaze but the flames didn't reach the makeshift roof. So far, so good.

She relaxed a little and spared a thought for Alfie and Mia, who had gone to collect driftwood from Echo

Cave Beach. 'I hope they're OK,' she murmured, making a promise to herself that she would never again wish for a storm. *Come back, clear skies and blue sea*, she thought. *Come back, dolphins!*

*

By midday, life on the island was back to normal.

The rain had stopped and the mists had cleared. A hot sun baked the wet sand.

Katie and James had watched the storm pass from the safety of the overhanging rock at Lookout Point before hurrying back to camp to check that all was well. Now James suggested that they spend the afternoon putting finishing touches to the new raft.

'The bamboo platform is finished,' he declared. 'All we need to do now is secure the flotation canisters, one at each corner.'

Over the weeks, the four plastic containers had been picked up from the shoreline at high tide. They'd been in the sea a long time, to judge by the faded labels, but luckily they'd been washed up complete with tops. The hope was that, with the tops firmly screwed on, the airtight canisters would be buoyant enough to keep the raft nicely afloat.

'It's amazing what the sea washes up.' Katie was in a chatty mood as she and Fleur tied the first container to the bamboo platform. 'Don't get me wrong – I'm not in favour of people polluting this beautiful ocean by chucking their rubbish overboard, but so far we've been able to make use of nearly every piece of flotsam and jetsam we come across.'

'Including these two planks of wood.' Alfie was hard at work with his new knife, whittling away at one of the smooth planks to shape it into a paddle. Meanwhile, James worked on the other.

'We've even used blobs of spilled oil to keep our torches alight.' Katie started on the second container. 'No one would have imagined that such nasty, gloopy black stuff would come in useful. It was your brilliant idea, Alfie.'

Alfie basked in his mum's praise. 'This raft is going to be cool,' he promised. 'It's loads bigger and better than the last one.'

'Meaning we can sail right around the island if we want to. Not to mention leaving for good, once we pluck up the courage.' Fleur looked forward to new adventures. 'So far we haven't explored the west coast. I wonder what we'll find there.'

'Different kinds of fruit trees,' Alfie suggested. 'Bananas maybe.'

'Dream on,' Fleur said with a smile. 'Melons would be good though – sweet, juicy yellow ones.'

'If this raft is as good as we hope, we'll soon find out.' James held up his paddle for inspection. 'What do you think, Mi-mi?'

She looked out from under the brim of her hat. 'Cool. What's it for?'

'To make the raft move faster.' He demonstrated by kneeling in the sand and miming the action. Then he pretended to overbalance and fall into the water. 'Splash!' he cried, kicking his legs in the air. 'Help, I can't swim!'

Mia laughed. 'Don't worry, Dad – Stormy will save you.'

'Talking of swimming,' her mum said, moving on to the next container, 'a little bird tells me you three snuck in a quick moonlit dip last night.' She picked up the third container and started to fix it in place.

Fleur flashed Alfie a quick look to see if it was worth attempting a big fib.

'The moon was pretty bright last night.' James stepped in before they could make up their minds. 'Your mum and I could see everything that was happening from the cliff path.'

'Ah.' Alfie realized they'd been caught red-handed. 'Sorry. I was excited to see Pearl. I forgot the rule.'

'Sorry,' Mia and Fleur mumbled without looking at their mum and dad.

'OK, we get it,' James said. 'You couldn't resist. In any case, if it was safe for your dolphins to come back into the bay, it was safe for you to be in the water with them.'

Fleur nodded. 'That's what we thought. Thanks, Dad.'

'But we still need to be careful in case the shark comes back,' Katie reminded them. 'You never know with those sneaky old tiger sharks, do you Mi-mi?'

Glad to escape a telling-off, Mia nodded solemnly and watched her mum lash the final container to the platform. She then checked that the top was screwed on tightly.

'OK – she's ready!' Katie announced. She stood back from the raft and looked down the beach. 'The water's calm right now. Shall we launch her?'

Eagerly Alfie and Fleur raised one end of the raft while Katie and James lifted the other. Mia ran ahead and waited impatiently at the water's edge.

'Steady as we go,' James instructed. 'Oops, we forgot the oars.' Letting Katie take the full weight of his end, he ran back to fetch them.

'Are you ready to lower her?' Katie asked Fleur and Alfie.

'Ready!' they said with mounting excitement. Slowly and carefully they set the raft down in the water where she bobbed gently in the shallow waves.

'Wait, we have to give her a name,' Alfie decided. 'What do we want to call her?'

'*Seagull*,' Mia suggested.

'Hmm – I quite like it,' Katie said.

'How about *Storm Petrel*?' Fleur asked.

'Not bad again,' was her mum's response. 'Alfie, what's your idea?'

He thought a while and decided to stick with a bird's

name. '*Sandpiper*.'

'Yes – I definitely like that,' James said, looking around the group. 'How about the rest of you?'

Mia, Fleur and Katie readily nodded their agreement.

'*Sandpiper* it is then,' James decided. 'OK, crew – are we ready to launch her?'

'Aye-aye, captain!' they cried as they gave mock salutes.

'Able Seaman Alfie, please do the honours.'

Alfie grinned from ear to ear. He stepped into the water and gave the raft a gentle shove as he made the official announcement. 'I name this raft *Sandpiper*!'

The brand-new raft drifted a few metres out to sea. All was going according to plan as the flotation aids tied to each corner kept the platform level and a few centimetres clear of the water.

'Who wants to be the first to sail in her?' James asked.

'Me! Me! Me!' Mia, Fleur and Alfie chorused loudly.

'OK, all three get on.' James handed an oar each to Fleur and Alfie. 'Your mum and I will hold her steady.'

So they waded out and clambered aboard – Fleur to

starboard and Alfie to port side while Mia stayed in the middle.

'Now start to paddle,' Katie instructed. 'Mia, sit still – don't fidget.'

Alfie and Fleur felt the raft tilt steeply to one side. The waves rose higher as they pointed out to sea.

'Paddle!' James cried from the shore.

'We're paddling!' Alfie and Fleur pushed hard with the oars without moving forward.

'Harder!' James cried.

'Uh-oh,' Katie muttered under her breath. It was obvious that a canister was letting in water and that *Sandpiper* was sinking. 'One of the tops must have come unscrewed!'

James too saw danger afoot. 'Besides which, the canisters aren't big enough to keep her clear of the water. Captain's orders – get ready to abandon ship!'

Centimetre by centimetre, the platform sank below the surface.

Mia, Fleur and Alfie sank with it into the cool water.

'Hop off – you're too heavy.' Katie grinned at the sight.

So the kids toppled sideways into the sea and the raft bobbed back into view.

'Hang on to your oars,' James told Fleur and Alfie as, laughing, he and Katie rushed into the water to save the raft. They managed to grab it before a current caught hold of it and carried it away.

'What's funny?' Fleur asked. She was dripping wet from head to toe. Her mum and dad were bent double.

'You three – you're funny,' James explained between bursts of laughter. 'You should've seen your faces when she started to sink.'

'After all that work!' Alfie cried. He waded out of the water and threw down his oar in disgust.

But laughter was infectious. Soon Fleur and Mia were grinning too. And eventually even Alfie couldn't resist – a smile crept on to his face. OK, so the grand naming ceremony and all the fanfare did seem funny, considering what had just happened.

'Back to the drawing board.' Katie helped James carry the raft to the shore.

'That's right – we're not giving up,' Alfie insisted as he waded in to lend a hand.

'What we need is more containers to keep her afloat. Bigger ones, if possible.' Fleur decided that she, Mia and Alfie would have to go beachcombing again to see what the morning storm had thrown up on to the beaches.

'That's the spirit,' their dad said happily. 'Think positive, kids. We've been through a lot since we got here, so making a seaworthy vessel is child's play compared with what we've achieved already.'

Chapter Seven

Saturday was a new day and Alfie was busily developing a new plan.

'Why are you looking so happy all of a sudden?' Fleur wondered. They were heading for Echo Cave with Mia in tow.

'I'm thinking about what Dad said yesterday – about making a seaworthy vessel.'

Fleur was puzzled. 'What's to think about? We agreed we need bigger containers, didn't we?' That was what they'd set off to look for straight after breakfast. Because of the direction of the currents off the east coast of Dolphin Island, the Fishers had quickly discovered that Echo Cave Beach was the ideal spot for beachcombing. Now it gave them the best chance of finding what they needed to keep *Sandpiper* afloat.

'He said "seaworthy vessel",' Alfie pointed out.

'Exactly.' Fleur walked on determinedly. Mia ran ahead as usual then stopped to perform cartwheels across the wet sand at the water's edge. 'I still don't get it, Alfie. That's what we're trying to do – make sure that *Sandpiper* doesn't sink next time.'

'"Vessel" doesn't mean just a raft, does it? It means cruise ships and paddle-steamers, oil-tankers, speedboats, yachts ...'

'Alfie.' She stepped across his path. 'What are you on about?'

'A vessel can be anything that floats, OK?' He swerved towards the shoreline, stooping to pick up a flat pebble then practise his skimming technique. 'Five bounces!' he declared proudly. 'Sure – a vessel can mean a raft. There was a famous one called *Kon-Tiki* – a Norwegian guy sailed thousands of miles around the world on it in the 1940s. We learned about him in geography – Thor Heyerdahl. He sailed her from South America to the Polynesian islands.'

'So what, Mister Navigation Expert?'

'Well, before I went to sleep last night, I was thinking

about the different types of things that float.'

Sometimes Alfie took ages to explain his ideas and it drove Fleur mad. 'OK – get to the point.'

He took no notice and carried on at his own slow, deliberate pace. 'A vessel can also mean a canoe.'

'A canoe?' she echoed. 'Why are we talking about canoes all of a sudden?'

Mia had reached the mouth of the cave and had already found a plastic waste bin and a bicycle inner tube amongst the seaweed and other rubbish. She held them up jubilantly for the others to see.

'Because I want to build one,' he said casually before stooping to skim another stone. One, two, three, four, five, six bounces!

There he went again – letting his imagination run wild on another hare-brained scheme. Fleur rolled her eyes. 'Yeah, yeah. How do you plan to do that?'

Alfie insisted that he had it all figured out. 'I'm not talking about a modern canoe made out of fibreglass,' he explained. 'I'm thinking more of an old-fashioned dugout canoe, like tribes on the Amazon used to use.'

'A dugout canoe?' This time she wasn't so quick to

mock. 'Made out of a hollowed-out tree trunk?'

'Yes – why not? There are plenty of fallen trees on this island. We could scout around until we find one the right size. And we have knives with sharp blades to do the hollowing out. That's more than the ancient tribes had. They probably just had stone flints.'

'OK, OK.' Fleur put her hands up to stop him before he got carried away. 'Are you saying that a canoe would be better than *Sandpiper*?'

Alfie shook his head. 'I'm not sure. But what's to stop us from building both? Or at least trying?'

'Trust you to dream big,' she muttered. But as she visualized it, the idea grew on her. It might not work out, but it would be fun to try. 'We'd need to find a suitable tree,' she pointed out.

'Easy-peasy,' he assured her, pointing towards the palm trees that fringed the beach. 'It'll be hard to do the hollowing out but I reckon if we all work together, we can do it.'

'Maybe.'

'Not maybe – definitely.' What was Fleur's problem? He'd worked it all out in his head and to him it all made perfect sense.

'I'll think about it,' she told him at last. 'I'm not saying yes to helping you make a canoe but I'm not saying no. Come on – let's go and see what Mia's up to.'

*

Over lunch-time and during their early afternoon siesta, Alfie gradually wore Fleur down.

'A canoe is tons better than a raft,' he insisted. 'It floats better for a start.'

'I thought you liked our raft,' she reminded him. 'It was you who collected most of the bamboo for it. You even chose her name.'

'I do like her. But we haven't managed to find any more canisters yet. *Sandpiper* won't float properly with the ones we've got. So at the moment we've got nothing to take us to the west side of the island – or use for our escape.'

'We could make *Sandpiper*'s platform smaller and lighter.'

'Then it would only be big enough for one person, like our first raft. And we're not allowed to go anywhere by ourselves, remember.'

Fleur lay on her back inside George's Cave, listening to the sound of the waves. Her pet gecko had perched on her stomach, patiently waiting to be fed. 'Fair enough,' she said with a sigh. She closed her eyes and tried to snooze.

'You don't get as wet in a canoe,' Alfie said after a short silence. 'You sit nice and snug inside it and the waves don't come in – whereas on a raft, you get splashed all the time.'

Fleur opened her eyes and stared at him. He sat in his grubby white T-shirt and red shorts, his legs stretched straight out and leaning back on his hands. 'You should know – you're the one who set off for Misty Island without telling anyone.'

'Yes, and look what happened.' On his way to the chain of islands off the southern point of Dolphin Island, he'd got caught in a major storm and the raft had broken up on a coral reef.

She kept on studying his face. 'You're not going to stop going on about it until I say yes, are you?'

'Nope.' He grinned back at her, his brown eyes shining.

She pretended to groan. Once Alfie had an idea, there was no limit to his pester-power. 'When would you want to start?'

'Now.' He jumped to his feet and stared down at her.

'We can't. The sun's scorching hot.'

'Later this afternoon then. What do you say?'

Fleur groaned again and gently shooed George on to the ground. Then she sat up and brushed sand from her arms and legs. 'OK,' she agreed as she stood up and looked him in the eye. 'You win. Let's go ahead and make your precious canoe.'

*

There was only one serious drawback to Alfie's plan – a suitable tree trunk proved hard to find.

'I thought it would be easier than this,' he admitted after he, Fleur and Mia had spent part of the afternoon searching and returned empty-handed to Base Camp Bay. They'd scoured the nearby beaches looking for fallen palm trees washed up by the tide, but the ones they'd found had been either too big, too small or else waterlogged from having floated on the sea for weeks on end. 'This is no good. I reckon we'll have to go up the mountain and search the forest instead.'

At first Fleur was dead set against the idea. 'No. It's too dark in there – we'd never be able to see.'

'I don't mean right in the middle of the forest,' Alfie argued. 'I'm talking about the edge.'

'No – too messy. You know what it's like in there – there'd be loads of creepers and bushes to cut down before we found something we could use.' She shuddered. No way did she want to go anywhere near the mountain-top jungle, not after what she'd seen and heard last time she was there.

Alfie gave her a sympathetic look to show that he understood. 'It's OK – Mia and I can do it. You don't need to come.'

'Honestly, Alfie – no. I don't think any of us should go into the forest.' Fleur's heart beat faster and her mouth went dry just thinking about it.

'Why not?' Mia chipped in. She saw everything as an exciting adventure and couldn't understand why Fleur was saying no.

'Because!' Fleur didn't want to scare her by

reminding her about the mystery creature.

But Mia wasn't listening. Instead, she seized Alfie by the hand and dragged him towards the cliff path. 'There's hundreds and hundreds of trees in the forest. We can easily find a good one for our canoe.'

Reluctantly Fleur decided for the second time that day that there was no point arguing and followed them up the cliff.

After a while, Alfie let Mia go on ahead. 'Don't worry,' he told Fleur. 'Nothing bad's going to happen. We'll only be in there long enough to find what we need.'

She swallowed hard. 'Maybe you're right,' she said quietly. But she still didn't like it, and as they crossed the open scrubland above Lookout Point, she grew more tense. 'Wait for us, Mi-mi!' she yelled up the slope. 'Don't go in there without us!'

For once, Mia obeyed.

'Really, you don't have to come,' Alfie repeated as he and Fleur reached the jackfruit tree, close to the point where the wild boar had fled from the forest. 'You can wait here if you like.'

'No, we have to stick together,' she said through

gritted teeth. '"All for one", remember?'

Alfie nodded. 'This will only take five minutes,' he promised.

So they climbed the hill and joined Mia. As they paused to catch their breath, they looked down at the brilliant, sparkling sea and at the fascinating patterns of dark and light turquoise patches formed by the coral reefs beneath. For a few moments Fleur pictured the underwater world of black and white striped parrotfish and wafting sea grass, of tiny, darting silversides and slow, ugly tarpon with their gaping mouths. And dolphins – always dolphins! Despite her fears, she smiled at the thought of Jazz, Pearl and Stormy cruising the blue ocean without a care.

'OK – ready?' Alfie asked.

She took a deep breath and nodded. 'I know the way better than you two. Let me go first.'

On they trod, out of the sunlight into the shadows. The air was hot and humid here, the atmosphere thick with buzzing insects and rustling leaves. All around there were vines looping down from thick branches and ferns sprouting up from the damp, dark earth. The tree trunks were green with moss and their bark was spongy to the touch.

'Can you see anything?' Mia whispered as their eyes grew used to the dark.

'Yes – lots of trees,' Fleur said with grim humour. Her forehead dripped with sweat and she almost tripped over tangled creepers that lay across her path.

'Look over there.' Alfie pointed to a medium-sized tree that had fallen and come to rest against its neighbour. 'How about that?'

'Too big and heavy,' Fleur decided. 'We'd never be able to carry it.'

Drops of moisture fell from the thick canopy of leaves above their heads and landed with loud splashes on the leaves below. Other than that, for once the forest was eerily silent.

'There's one!' Mia spotted a smaller tree lying on the ground and Alfie ventured over to examine it.

He picked up a short stick and poked the trunk. 'It's rotten,' he reported as soft pieces of wood crumbled under his touch. 'Look – it's got giant yellow toadstools growing from it.'

'Don't touch them in case they're poisonous,' Fleur warned. There was a rustle behind her and she jumped, almost losing her footing. She couldn't wait to get out of the forest. Forcing herself to focus, she looked further ahead and spotted a third fallen tree. She made her way towards it and carefully cleared away some of the undergrowth. 'This one's not rotten,' she told the others.

They soon joined her and inspected her find. 'It looks OK,' Alfie agreed. He saw that the tree's shallow roots had been torn away as it fell, making it easy to move, and that it was about the right length for them to carry. 'Let's try.'

'Wait a second.' Fleur cleared away more creepers. 'OK, ready,' she said as she took a firm hold of the thick end of the trunk.

With Mia in the middle and Alfie at the other end, they tried to raise the small tree from the ground.

'Oof!' Mia grunted, as they failed to lift it a single centimetre.

Alfie thought fast. 'OK, we'll have to tie creepers around it and try to drag it.'

He and Fleur worked quickly to do this. 'Grab the end of this one, Mi-mi,' Alfie instructed when they'd finished.

All three took the strain, ready to heave the tree along the ground.

'Ready?' Alfie asked.

They pulled with all their might. Slowly but surely they began to edge their way forward.

Suddenly the silent forest came alive. Two rats scuttled out from under the fallen trunk and a flightless cassowary darted out of a nearby bush, its white head bobbing as it ran close to the ground to take refuge behind a boulder. Overhead, three tree kangaroos swung swiftly from branch to branch. Somewhere, out of sight, cockatoos shrieked.

'Ignore them. Keep going,' Fleur told the others. She hoped that moving the tree was what had caused the disturbance, not the approach of some deadly creature. They were less than thirty metres from the edge of the forest, but she wasn't sure that they would make it.

'Sunlight ahead!' Alfie called over his shoulder, pausing to choose the best way forward. He took care not to trip and not to go too fast for Mia to keep up.

'Stop. My eyes are stinging.' Without warning Mia let go of her improvised rope to wipe sweat from her forehead.

Fleur and Afie took the full weight of their burden until she was ready to go on. Twenty metres and then ten – one step at a time.

'Not long now,' Alfie promised. Warm shafts of light fell across his path. He could see white butterflies ahead against blue sky and at last they emerged into sunlight. He, like Fleur, breathed an enormous sigh of relief. 'Cool – we did it!' he cried.

Chapter Eight

That night Mia, Alfie and Fleur slept soundly.

'It must be all that hard work you did yesterday, pulling the tree down the mountain,' James told them as, for once, he had to wake them all up.

He'd been surprised to see Mia, Fleur and Alfie arrive at camp at sunset, their faces smeared with dirt and sweat, having lugged a whole tree down from the forest. He'd sent them for a quick swim to get clean before supper then he'd listened to their excited chatter over a meal of smoked fish and baked yucca root.

'Hang on a minute,' he'd said when he'd examined the tree then picked up the gist of their conversation. 'What's this I hear about a boat?'

They'd all jumped in at once with excited explanations.

'A dugout canoe,' Alfie had told him.

'A boat that floats,' Mia had clamoured. 'Hey, that rhymes!'

'Big enough for two people,' Fleur had added as if it was the simplest, most obvious thing in the world.

They'd gone on discussing their plans by the campfire as darkness fell, and hadn't stopped even at bedtime. In the end James had been forced to ask them to pipe down and get some shut-eye.

'They're making a canoe,' James had informed Katie when she came down from Lookout Point after building up the fire.

Katie had looked surprised. 'I saw them pulling the tree down the mountain, but I had no idea what they planned to do with it.'

'I hope they haven't bitten off more than they can chew,' he'd said quietly as he and Katie made sure the camp was shipshape before they too went to bed.

'Whose idea was it – Alfie's?'

'How did you guess? Fleur and Mia have promised to help. They're dead set on doing it.'

'So good luck to them.' Katie was proud of her

children and if they managed to pull this off she would be even more so.

Still, the longer she and James thought about it, the more convinced they grew that the task ahead was too big to handle.

*

'Where do we start?' Fleur asked Alfie as they emerged from the shelter and took a fresh look at the tree.

'First we have to hack off the branches,' he decided, striding over to the ledge next to the food store where they kept their knives. 'What we really need is a saw, but I reckon this will have to do.' He held up the knife with the serrated edge, rescued from *Merlin* before she sank.

Fleur remembered what he'd said about the old tribes using flints. 'What if I go and search at the bottom of the cliff for sharp stones?' she suggested.

'Cool.'

'Me too,' Mia decided.

Without delay, the girls pushed their way through the bushes and began the hunt for objects that could be used as tools to carve through wood.

'Is this sharp enough?' Mia asked, holding up a flat stone that was loose on the ground. 'Or this one?'

Neither was any good but Fleur didn't have the heart to say so. 'I'll tell you what: let's make a pile here on this flat piece of rock and take them back when we think we've collected enough.'

What they really needed was actual flints – really hard, thin shards that had split away from rocks and could be shaped into arrow-heads or spears, the same as the ones Stone Age man had used. What they didn't need was what Mia kept on finding – soft rocks that would crumble or smooth pebbles with rounded edges. Fleur paused and glanced up the cliff face to see a fat, blue-grey pigeon perched on a ledge and staring down at her. 'I know,' she muttered as if the bird had asked what on earth she thought she was doing. 'I'm beginning to wonder that myself.'

The pigeon soon lost interest and shuffled out of sight.

'How about this?' Mia asked, showing her a sliver of brown stone edged with a thin layer of white.

'Put it on the pile,' Fleur said with a sigh. Then she

had second thoughts. 'No – wait a minute. Let me take a proper look.'

Mia handed her the stone.

Fleur held it in her palm and turned it over. She looked at it from every angle. The surface was smooth and shiny; the edges were razor sharp.

'Wow – good girl! This is exactly what we're looking for.' It was flint – real flint that must have lain at the bottom of the cliff for thousands, maybe millions of years. 'Keep on looking, Mi-mi. See how many stones like this we can find.'

*

Chip-chip-chip. It was several hours later and Mia and Fleur were working away at the tree trunk with their precious pieces of flint while Alfie sawed at the branches. They'd been at it all day, only stopping to eat and do the basic chores of fetching water and keeping the fires going.

'I've got a blister,' Mia complained towards the end of the afternoon. She held up her hand to show them a sore spot at the base of her thumb.

'That's OK – you can stop for a bit if you like.' Alfie

straightened up to ease the crick in his back.

'Go for a paddle,' Fleur suggested. 'But don't go out of your depth.'

Mia was off like a shot, down the beach and into the water where she splashed away happily.

Fleur watched her dash off then took a step back. By using a heavy, blunt stone as a hammer to tap the sharp flint, she'd made a groove in the tree trunk about fifty centimetres long, ten centimetres wide and roughly five centimetres deep. 'You know what – this is going to take for ever,' she complained.

'You're right.' Alfie too felt discouraged. So far he'd only managed to hack off two of the branches. Already the knife was blunt. 'I was thinking – I might know a quicker way to do the hollowing out part. I saw it on a TV programme once.'

'*Now* he tells us!' Examining her own hands, Fleur rubbed at a sore spot and frowned.

'It was pretty cool, actually. This tribe that lived by the Amazon – they set fire to a section of the trunk then allowed the flames to burn through the wood. But they put the fire out at just the right time, before it had a chance to burn all the way through. Then they set light to the next section and did it all over again. In the end they had a row of burnt-out hollows all the way along. Then they just had to finish off with an axe or a chisel.'

'Fire?' Fleur looked at him aghast. 'You can't be serious.'

'What's wrong with that? It'd be a lot quicker than this method, that's for sure.'

'But fire, Alfie?' Fleur gestured at their shelter and all their belongings. 'What if it ran out of control? We'd lose everything.'

'We already keep the campfire alight all day long,' he pointed out. 'And that's even closer to the shelter.'

'That's true,' she admitted. 'But honestly I still think it's too risky. This is only the end of our first day of working on the canoe, remember. Let's carry on like this for a few more days – see how far we get.'

He nodded. 'Anyway, just think how cool it will be to have a boat to take us past Black Crab Cove. I spotted a mangrove swamp down at the southern tip of the island. We can paddle the canoe in there, amongst the weird, twisted roots. We'll be able to explore places we've never been to before then mark them on the map.'

'Yes and I'm looking forward to paddling under the rock arch off Black Crab Cove.' His enthusiasm was infectious and Fleur grinned at him. 'Listen; I'm sorry about yesterday.'

'What are you sorry for?' Ready to take a rest, Alfie put down the knife and they sat together on the sand.

She pushed her wavy brown hair back from her face and crossed her legs. 'For being stupid and making a fuss about going into the forest. It turned out fine so I'm glad you made me do it.'

'It's OK – I get it.' He turned his face towards the low sun in the west, closed his eyes and soaked up its warm rays. 'I wasn't there when the boar thing happened – you were. I'd have been scared too if I'd been you.'

She traced a zigzag pattern in the sand with her flint. 'I still don't know what made them run,' she reminded him. 'But this Creature, whatever it was, was pretty big – I could tell that that by the way it moved.'

Fleur said the word 'Creature' as if it began with a capital letter because that was how she imagined it – a thing of dark mystery and cruelty.

'How?'

'Slow and heavy.'

Alfie persisted with his questions. He wanted a firmer idea of what she had in mind. 'As big as an elephant, say?'

'No, that would be impossible.' She drew her initials in the sand – FMF for Fleur Molly Fisher. 'It can't be an elephant, can it? They always go about in herds. This was just one Creature.'

'A bear then?'

She shook her head. 'You don't get bears around here either. And not a lion or a tiger or anything like that.'

'How do you know?'

'This thing didn't growl or roar – it hissed.'

Alfie thought about the skeleton they'd found then opened his eyes and looked steadily at Fleur. 'This animal – whatever it is – do you reckon it killed the boar?'

She nodded slowly. 'That's another thing that makes me think I was right to be freaked out.'

'It must be really big,' he added, 'if it hunts wild boar.'

They sat in silence, their faces serious. 'Don't say anything to Mia,' Fleur said after a while. She'd noticed their little sister setting back up the beach at the same time as their mum and dad appeared on the southern headland, returning from a fishing trip to Turtle Beach.

'OK,' he agreed. Their conversation had unsettled him more than he'd expected. 'She'd be spooked big time. What about Mum and Dad?'

Fleur shook her head. 'No. What's the point? They'd only worry.'

'*I* worry!' Alfie confessed. He sighed and stood up. 'What if this jungle monster thingy creeps out of the forest during the night and makes a tasty supper out of one of us?'

'Alfie – don't! Thinking about the Creature already keeps me awake at night. Let's forget about it – OK?'

He pressed his lips together and drew his forefinger and thumb across his mouth. 'Zzzip!'

'Thanks.' Fleur swept her hand across the sand and rubbed out her initials. 'I'm hoping it stays deep in the forest from now on and we never see it again.'

'Let's hope,' he agreed. He looked up towards the dark mountain. The peak was shrouded by white mist while the sky all around was a fierce orange. Nearer at hand, a row of marauding macaques sat silently on a cliff ledge, waiting for an opportunity to steal into camp.

'Shoo!' Alfie got over his surprise and shook his fist at them. 'Go on – scoot!'

The monkeys refused to budge. In fact, the biggest one picked up a stone and threw it at him. The stone landed harmlessly in the bushes.

'Missed!' Alfie cried.

'Did you see that?' Fleur rushed to join him. 'The alpha male used a missile to attack us. How clever was that?'

Alfie frowned and set off up the cliff path, determined to show the pesky creatures that he meant business. 'You won't be saying that when they steal our food. I mean it, you monkeys – shoo, scram, get out of here!'

'What's Alfie doing?' Mia asked as she arrived back at camp, smiling and dripping wet.

'Chasing poor little macaques.' Fleur returned her smile. 'Don't worry – he won't catch them.'

The monkeys waited on the shadowy ledge until Alfie drew near. Their pale bellies and white eyelids showed up in the dark; their eyes glittered. When Alfie was almost close enough to reach out and touch the nearest one, they bared their teeth.

'Careful, Alfie!' James's voice drifted up the beach. 'There's five of them and only one of you.'

'Go and eat someone else's food.' Breathless from the climb, Alfie drew level with the invaders. 'There are hundreds of gulls' eggs everywhere you look. There are crabs in the rock pools – lots of yummy stuff.'

Their curious faces stared back at him.

'How come you're so fearless?' he wanted to know. 'Why aren't you running away?'

They tilted their heads from side to side as if considering their next move.

'Go away, monkeys!' Mia yelled from down below.

'Wait – I've got an idea. Stay back, Mi-mi.' Carefully

Fleur shielded her face from the heat and approached the campfire. She leaned forward and very gingerly drew out a long, flaming branch. Then, brandishing it in front of her with her arm outstretched, she followed Alfie up the cliff. The branch flickered and gave off sparks. Smoke spiralled through the air and soon reached the monkeys' nostrils.

'Good thinking.' Alfie watched the monkeys react nervously to the strange smell and start to back off along the ledge. 'It seems to be working.'

Fleur soon joined him and passed the burning branch to him. He jabbed it towards the macaques, who turned in a flash and were gone from the ledge and up the cliff, leaping from rock to rock until they disappeared from sight.

'Good job!' Alfie grinned at Fleur and they high-fived.

Down on the beach, their mum and dad called for them to return. 'We caught eels for supper and we saw turtles,' James told them. 'Your mum found more sugarcane.'

'Mmm – delicious.' Trusting Alfie to carry the

branch, Fleur led the way down the cliff. She looked forward to eels fried in coconut oil and chunks of chewy, sweet sugarcane. They'd made a start on the boat and would work on it again tomorrow. Hopeful as always, she glanced out to sea – Jazz and the others had stayed away, but apart from that, Day 35 had turned out to be a pretty good day.

Chapter Nine

The following morning, Jazz, Stormy and Pearl showed up bright and early in Base Camp Bay.

Mia had only just marked the calendar stick and Fleur and Alfie were standing by the beginnings of their boat. They rubbed sleep from their eyes and assessed the small amount of progress they'd made on their big new project, not noticing the three young dolphins approaching the shore.

Mia spotted them first and called for the others. 'Hurry up – time for a swim.'

No sooner said than all three were racing down the beach and flinging themselves into the water. They swam front crawl towards the reef, laughing when the dolphins circled around them and gave small, welcoming yelps. Then they slapped their tail flukes on the surface and sent spray high into the air.

Half drowned by the heavy spray, Alfie reached out and stroked Pearl's head. Then he dived underneath her pink belly and came up on the far side waving a piece of brown seaweed at her. She lunged towards it and took it between her teeth, dragging it further out to sea before shaking her head and flinging it high in the air.

Stormy joined in the game. He sped through the water and caught the seaweed then leaped clear of the surface and spun in midair before tossing it in Jazz's direction. Jazz the acrobat cleared the water and caught it with ease.

Mia and Fleur cheered them on. 'Good catch, Stormy! You go, Jazz!'

Alfie kicked hard and followed Jazz in an arc across the bay. 'Slow down,' he pleaded. 'I'm nowhere near as fast as you guys.'

Jazz seemed to understand. With the seaweed clamped between his jaws, he turned on his back and scudded gently with his flippers until Alfie was within arm's length. Then, as if to tease him, he twisted on to his belly and shot off again.

Laughing loudly and cheering Jazz on, Fleur and Mia tried to cut him off, but it was Pearl and Stormy who sped ahead to crowd in on him and challenge him for the seaweed. Jazz made the mistake of opening his jaws to give off a warning yelp and the seaweed slipped from his mouth and sank out of sight.

'Boo!' Mia cried as the team game ended and the dolphins swam back towards them. 'That was fun.'

Jazz squeaked loudly as he rejoined Fleur. Pearl chirped and whistled while Stormy splashed with his tail and rattled off a series of rapid clicks.

'Come on – let's have a group hug before you go,' Fleur declared. She put one arm around Jazz and the other around Pearl, while Alfie and Mia completed the circle by putting their arms around Pearl and Stormy. They trod water in the middle of the bay as the sun rose higher in the misty pink sky. The dolphins' skin felt soft and velvety to the touch. Their wide, upturned mouths seemed to smile.

'OK – time for you three to go find fish.' Alfie was the one to break the happy circle and send Pearl,

Stormy and Jazz on their way. 'And time for us to work on the boat,' he told Fleur and Mia eagerly.

'Breakfast first.' Fleur let go of Jazz after one final hug.

As the dolphins swam rapidly out past the reef, she, Mia and Alfie made their much slower way towards the shore. They waded out of the water then turned for a last glimpse of their dolphins heading for the shimmering horizon.

'Bye for now,' Fleur murmured. Alfie dashed ahead towards the shelter, while she held hands with Mia and wandered slowly up the beach.

*

'Who wants to work on the raft with me and Dad and who wants to work on the boat?' was Katie's question after they'd eaten their fill of scrambled eggs and slices of jackfruit.

'Raft!' Mia cried without hesitating.

'Boat,' Fleur and Alfie decided.

'OK, Mia – our first job is to carry on beachcombing. We're heading for Turtle Beach today to look for more of those big canisters.' James set Mia's sunhat firmly on her head. 'If we don't find any there, we'll carry on to Pirate Cave Beach and search there.'

'Don't worry about us if we're not back for lunch,' Katie told the other two, holding up their home-made rucksack. 'We're taking food and water with us.'

Fleur wished them luck as they prepared to set off. 'We'll be here all day in any case.'

'Remember to feed the fires,' James reminded them. 'Oh, and we'll need more fresh water. Put that on your list.'

As the small team of raft-builders set off towards the headland, Fleur and Alfie settled down to work. Alfie had the bright idea of trying to sharpen his knife by rubbing the sides of the blade against a hard, smooth rock while Fleur decided to protect her sore hand by bandaging it with strips of dried palm leaf. This meant that the sun had risen to half its height before they'd properly begun.

'This is really tough.' Alfie breathed hard as he sawed at a branch until finally he cut all the way through. He was already sweating and in need of a rest.

Meanwhile, Fleur chipped away with her flint. As

she worked on, her mind was busy with a dozen different things – a promise to herself that she would enjoy a piece of sugarcane after lunch, which led to a memory of one of her favourite puddings back home – chocolate sponge with custard – followed by a fleeting thought about the Creature that darted into her consciousness out of nowhere. *Don't!* she told herself, repressing a shudder. *Think about nice stuff like strawberry and mango smoothies.* She hunched forward over the tree trunk and chipped without stopping while the sun beat down on her back.

Alfie picked up one end of the branch he'd sawn off and dragged it towards the woodpile. He knew it would make good firewood after it had dried out. While he was there, he took two pieces of driftwood and fed the campfire. 'That reminds me,' he told Fleur. 'I'd better go up to Lookout Point and chuck some more wood on the fire.'

'I'll come.' Fleur was glad to put down her flint. She unwrapped the palm leaf bandage then went into the shelter and brought out two empty water bottles. 'We'll fill these on the way back.'

So they climbed the cliff path and reached the lookout, where they rested and took in deep breaths of fresh air.

'Let's not rush back,' Fleur said, choosing a shaded spot upwind of the fire to sit down and dangle her legs over the edge of the ledge. 'There's a nice breeze and the colour of the sea from up here is amazing.'

Alfie piled wood on the fire then joined her to enjoy the bird's eye view. 'I wonder if the others have found any containers yet.'

'Who knows? But in any case, I bet you anything that *Sandpiper* is ready to set sail before our boat is.'

'How much?' Alfie wasn't ready to concede defeat on the boat-building challenge. 'OK, I bet you a ...' He had to think hard about what they could wager. '... A giant conch shell that we beat them to it.'

Fleur grinned and shook his hand. 'Deal!'

They were laughing about their bet and admitting that neither actually owned a giant conch when Alfie's attention was caught by movements in the bushes that fringed the beach below. He and Fleur were too high up to hear any sounds but soon he saw the leaves part and the moustachioed face of a macaque monkey peer out. 'Uh-oh,' he muttered, jabbing Fleur with his elbow. 'Down there in the bushes behind the shelter – take a look.'

'Uh-oh,' she echoed then gave a loud groan.

A second face appeared and then a third. As soon as the monkeys were sure that the camp was deserted, they crept out on to the beach.

'Come on – the pests are back and they're after our food.' Alfie swung himself down from the ledge on to the cliff path and set off at a run.

Fleur followed, working out, even if they kept on running, it would take them at least ten minutes to reach Base Camp. The way down was steep and for a while she lost sight of the monkeys. It was only when she joined Alfie at Butterfly Falls that she saw them again.

The smallest of the three was perched on the roof of their shelter with a ringside view of what the other two were up to. The middle one – an adult female – ran on all fours, her long tail twitching as she peered into the empty shelter and then quickly skirted the campfire to join the male leader of the trio who was picking at the canvas cover to their food store.

'Hey, don't do that!' Alfie's outraged cry rang out. 'Leave our food alone!'

This time Fleur took the lead as they left the waterfall and scrambled on down the steep path. By now all three monkeys had grouped together and begun to tug at the canvas sheet that covered their food store. Unable to shift it, they soon remembered that the canvas was weighted down by big rocks and it didn't take them long to start pushing the rocks to one side. Within seconds, they'd dragged the canvas cover clear of the dried fish, nuts and fruit stored beneath it.

Out of breath after their hurried descent, Fleur watched the female macaque and the youngster sink their teeth into the nearest juicy jackfruit and groaned again. 'It's no good – we're too late.'

Alfie frowned and muttered angrily under his breath.

Instead of raiding the store with the other two, the big male seemed fascinated by the piece of frayed, dirty canvas that they'd pulled loose. First he jumped on it then pounded it with his fists before he seized one edge and began to drag it across the sand. He stopped and flapped it from side to side then picked it up and swung it clumsily around his head like a flag, suddenly letting go of it in mid-swing. Alfie and Fleur saw it sail through the air and land on the fire. They watched in horror as flames flared up around the bone-dry canvas.

'This is bad,' Alfie groaned. 'Really bad!'

Within seconds the canvas was blazing and a wind blew the flames in the direction of the shelter. Caught in an unexpected blast of heat, the three terrified culprits squealed and fled.

Helpless from their position halfway up the cliff, Fleur and Alfie continued to watch.

Sparks danced upwards from the greedy flames. Carried by the wind, they landed on the top of the shelter where they glowed red then quickly ignited. Soon the whole roof was alight, the woven palm leaves burning fiercely as the flames raged on, destroying everything in their path.

Alfie closed his eyes. He felt sick at the sight. Fleur

gave a strangled cry as the whole of their shelter and all of its contents burned down before her eyes – their map of the island, the calendar stick, their beds, insect screen – all gone!

By now the roaring fire was unstoppable. It crept towards the bushes and flared up afresh. Flames reached high into the palm tree canopy and soon this too was ablaze. They spread in all directions – from the embers of the ruined shelter, back down the beach to the family's store of rope, plastic bags and bottles. Black smoke billowed as they set alight and then, seconds later, *Sandpiper* was gobbled up by the flames. The bamboo platform disintegrated quickly and was left in smoking ruins. Nothing survived.

And now the crackling, spitting fire spread up the hillside, fanned by the wind. It set light to every bush in its path, causing clouds of blue smoke to rise high into the air.

Fleur turned to Alfie in fresh panic. 'Open your eyes!' she hissed as she tugged his arm. 'Alfie, we have to move!'

He forced himself to look down at a scene of total

destruction. Flames everywhere – everything gone. A sob caught in his throat as he let her drag him towards the waterfall where they doused themselves in water.

'Take off your T-shirt,' Fleur told him as she did the same and showed him how to tie it around his nose and mouth to form a damp, protective mask. 'Otherwise we could choke to death.'

He nodded, his eyes wide with fear. The smoke grew thicker still as the flames set fire to yet more scrubland. 'At this rate the whole island will burn down. What now?' he cried.

'We have to get as far away as possible,' she insisted. Their voices came out muffled from behind their masks. 'We can't use the cliff path any more, so we'll have to figure out a new way to reach the beach and pick a spot by the water where the flames can't reach us.'

'We could try that way, upwind of the fire?' With a desperate, choking cry, Alfie pointed to a stretch of land to the south of Lookout Point where the land fell away steeply.

Fleur agreed and they began to pick their way between rocks, clinging on to bushes and sliding down the gravel surface on their bottoms. They prayed that the wind would keep a steady course, blowing in from the sea and driving the flames north-west across the scrubland leading to the forest.

Almost at the bottom of the slope, Fleur slipped and grazed her elbow. In her panic, she hardly noticed that the wound immediately started to bleed.

'Hurry!' Alfie urged. 'It gets steeper here. We might have to jump the last bit.'

She bit her lip and fought back tears. 'What about the animals?' she murmured, glancing back up the hillside. The birds on the island would be OK because they could fly off, but what about the tree kangaroos and the possums, the geckos, the rats and bats and wild boars? What about the monkeys themselves?

'Fleur, we have to hurry!' Alfie insisted.

She drew breath and slithered down the slope to join him. Together they looked at a sheer three-metre drop on to the beach.

'Ready, steady, go!' he shouted.

Fleur and Alfie launched themselves through the air and landed in the soft, dry sand.

Chapter Ten

Over at Pirate Cave Beach, Mia crawled on her belly through the low entrance into the cave that she and Alfie had explored soon after they'd arrived on Dolphin Island. Once inside, there was plenty of room to stand up and look around.

Katie and James had to wait outside. 'No way can we grown-ups wriggle through there.' Her dad had taken one look at the low, overhanging rock before deciding he would get stuck halfway. 'It's all up to you, Mi-mi. Can you see anything?'

'Not much,' she replied, waiting for her eyes to grow used to the dark. 'But listen to this.' She cupped her hands around her mouth. 'Whoo-oo-ooh!'

'Whoo-oo-ooh!' Her voice came echoing back.

'Who's there?' she called.

'Who's there-there-there?'

'No time for messing about, Mia.' Katie lay flat and peered into the cave. 'We're looking for big plastic containers, remember.'

Mia poked at a pile of broken shells and dried seaweed that the waves had flung into the cave during the last storm. 'Yuck!' Flies rose from the rotting pile and buzzed around her head. She held her breath then stooped to pick up a crushed can and an old foam-rubber cushion. Backing away from the heap of rubbish, she breathed again and reported her find.

'OK – bring the cushion with you,' James decided. 'It might come in useful.'

'Anything else?' Katie asked.

Mia looked all round the cave, especially in the crevices between the rocks where, amongst the broken shells and dried seaweed, she came across an old pair of glasses, a blue plastic sack and another rusty can. She put the glasses into her pocket but decided to leave the sack and the can behind because they already had plenty back at camp. 'It smells horrid in there,' she told Katie and James, wrinkling her nose as she squirmed back out. She'd flung the cushion out ahead of her and now delved in her pocket to drag out the glasses.

'Talking of bad smells ...' James sniffed the air.

Katie and Mia concentrated on the glasses. 'One lens is broken but the other is fine,' Katie said. 'I reckon this will come in very handy if we ever have to light a new fire.'

'How?' Mia wanted to know.

Katie's answer was slow and patient. 'Well, we make a heap of twigs and dried grass on the ground. We hold the lens over the heap. Then the sun shines down through the lens. That makes the rays get really, really intense so the kindling heats up until it bursts into flames.'

'Wow! Is it magic?'

'Kind of,' Katie said with a smile. 'Anyway, well done, Mi-mi.'

Mia smiled proudly, spotted another pile of rubbish closer to the water's edge and dashed off to take a look. Katie followed more slowly.

'Yes, that's it – I smell smoke!' James said with knotted brows. He walked down the beach after the others, sniffing and frowning as he went.

'Yay!' Mia cried, seizing one end of a long piece of orange rope and dragging it free from the new heap of debris. Trailing it behind her, she ran to show James her latest find.

'What?' Instead of paying attention, he glanced the other way, towards the mountain. 'Hmm, that's good, Mi-mi. Well done.'

'Dad,' she insisted as she thrust the end of the rope under his nose. 'You're not looking.'

'Smoke,' he repeated quietly. Then he gasped when he saw thick blue plumes rising from the hillside. 'Katie!' he yelled. 'Fire! Fire on the mountain!'

Katie followed his pointing finger and saw the smoke. Her heart missed a beat as she realized what it meant. 'Oh, no – this can't be happening!'

'Hurry. We've got to get back to camp as fast as we can.' Without waiting for Katie and Mia, James took the lead over the rocks on to Turtle Beach.

Katie took Mia's hand and they struggled to keep up. With his long legs, James was already halfway across the neighbouring beach when they jumped down from the headland. He sprinted on towards Base Camp Bay. The smoke was growing thicker and now they could see wildfire rampaging up the slope above Lookout Point. Katie's heart missed another beat at the first sight of the yellow and orange flames leaping from bush to bush across the open expanse.

'Mummy – where are Alfie and Fleur?' Mia asked, her voice breaking down as she spoke.

'Don't worry – we'll find them.' Katie held on to her hand and hid her own fear. This was a disaster – the whole hillside was ablaze and they had absolutely no idea where Fleur and Alfie had been when the fire had started.

They all ran as hard as they could through the soft sand with only one desperate thought whirling around their heads – *Fleur and Alfie, Fleur and Alfie, Fleur and Alfie!*

*

Safe on the beach at Base Camp Bay, Fleur winced as she touched the skin on her injured elbow. When she took her hand away she saw that her fingers were covered in blood.

137

Alfie took off his mask, shook out the folded T-shirt then put it on. He drew a deep breath. OK, so they'd made it down the cliff, but what did they do next? Hadn't they better go and find the others and tell them what had happened? He turned to check with Fleur and saw that she was bleeding. 'That looks bad,' he groaned. 'Does it hurt?'

'A bit.' With clumsy, trembling fingers Fleur untied her T-shirt, scrunched it into a ball then used it to mop up the blood. She was more worried about the animals in the forest than the graze on her arm. It was crystal-clear that she and Alfie could do nothing to stop the fire – it had raged on, away from the smoking remains of the camp, up the cliff face towards the forest. All they could do was hope that by some miracle the flames stopped short of the trees.

'Let me see,' Alfie insisted.

So she raised the bloodstained T-shirt and showed him.

'It's got dirt and pieces of grit in it,' he realized. 'You need to wash it.'

She pulled back. 'Not right now. What about the

monkeys and the wild boar – everything that lives in the forest? What's going to happen to them?' Then she was struck by another dreadful thought. 'And what about George?'

Before he could stop her, she'd thrown down her T-shirt and sprinted off towards camp, only coming to a halt when she reached the burnt-out shelter. Thin spirals of smoke rose from the heap of glowing ashes. The slender palm trees that had once shielded their camp from the wind had turned into charred, bare columns. Even the rocks were blackened by smoke.

'George, where are you?' Fleur wailed. 'Wait a minute. Maybe, just maybe ...' Holding her breath, she set off again; this time towards her pet gecko's cave. She reached the entrance and looked anxiously inside.

There he was, squatting on his ledge, calmly staring back at her.

'Oh, thank goodness!' Fleur found she could breathe again. She showed Alfie where George had taken refuge. 'I don't know what I'd have done if—'

'Don't even think about it.' Alfie cut her off and

looked back at the mountain to see that the fire was still making rapid progress. The trees on the summit were already shrouded in thick smoke and the flames crept steadily closer. 'Listen, we have to find the others,' he decided, setting off along the shoreline.

Fleur agreed. 'Stay there, George.'

Still as a statue, the gecko didn't move a muscle.

So she ran after Alfie, wading after him into the water then plunging in deeper to swim around the headland into Turtle Bay.

'This will be quicker than climbing the headland,' he yelled back.

She swam as fast as she could against a strong undertow, making sure to steer clear of the sharp rocks. The salt water made her elbow sting but at least that meant her wound would be cleaned. 'Mum and Dad are bound to have seen the smoke by now,' she called to Alfie. She took in a mouthful of salt water as she spoke then spat it out. 'They'll be heading home, wondering what on earth's going on.'

'Big jellyfish – watch out!' he warned as he made a detour further out to sea to avoid its pulsating, transparent body and floating tentacles.

Fleur followed him through a patch of sea grass growing from a coral reef just below the surface. Beyond the headland the current wasn't so strong and the incoming tide swept them towards the shore. Before long they were able to touch sand with the soles of their feet, then start wading towards the beach.

'OK?' Making sure that Fleur was still close behind him, Alfie noticed that her wet arm was streaked with blood. 'Your elbow's still bleeding.'

'Yes, but it doesn't matter.' A quick glance showed that a lot of the dirt had come out in the water.

'Here – borrow this.' Alfie had taken off his T-shirt again and offered it to Fleur before she could say no. As he waited for her to wrap it around her arm to stem the flow of blood, he glanced back the way they'd come. What he saw a few metres offshore sent a fresh shiver down his spine.

'What is it, Alfie?' Fleur saw him start and tremble.

Without saying a word, he grabbed her arm and tried to run, looking over his shoulder to check that he wasn't mistaken.

The shark was back. Its whole body was visible above the surface, from its massive, blunt snout to the tip of its long, pointed tail; a dark blue killing machine with tiger stripes on its back. It cruised towards them in a straight line, all four metres of it, swinging its tail fluke from side to side and opening its ferocious jaws.

Blood. Fleur's blood. The tiger shark had been lurking far out to sea. The moment she and Alfie had entered the water, it had picked up the vibrations that their bodies had made in the water and then detected the flow of blood from Fleur's elbow wound. It had honed in on the smell and tracked them down with incredible speed. Now here it was, metres from the shore, watching and waiting.

Now Fleur saw it too. She cried out, stumbled and almost overbalanced. 'Hurry, we have to get out of the water!'

Together they waded swiftly, praying that the shark wouldn't overtake them before they reached the shore.

'How long has it been back in our waters?' Fleur gasped.

'Who knows? We'll have to warn everyone not

to go swimming again.'

The shark came closer still, displaying its vicious teeth. Horrified, they splashed on through the shallows, chests taut with fear. Only a few metres separated them from the tiger shark's wide jaws. Then, suddenly and without warning, it switched direction with a sudden flick of its tail and put on a burst of speed back out to sea.

For a few brief seconds, relief flooded through Alfie and Fleur until they realized what had made the shark change its mind. For there, beyond the reef, were their three very own dolphins, rising out of the water, arching through the air and splashing back down as if they were deliberately trying to attract the enemy's attention.

There was no mistake – Stormy, Jazz and Pearl were daring the shark to chase them and hunt them down, acting as decoys to allow Fleur and Alfie to escape its jaws.

'No – we're OK! Get out of here!' Alfie and Fleur called out at the tops of their voices.

The shark forgot about the scent of blood that had

drawn it to the shore. Now its fin sliced through the calm surface until it drew level with the reef.

'Go! Go!' they cried.

The dolphins waited until the last possible moment then they sped away. They swam out to sea ahead of the shark, criss-crossing the open water, still teasing and tempting it with spectacular leaps and twists.

Unable to watch the deadly game, Fleur turned away. Alfie clenched his fists in front of him and silently urged Pearl, Stormy and Jazz onwards until at last they all made one mighty, final leap and disappeared beneath the waves. The shark dived down after them and then all was still.

*

Halfway across Turtle Beach James's legs almost gave out. His lungs ached. But he wouldn't stop running until he found out what had happened to Fleur and Alfie.

Not far behind, Katie and Mia struggled on. High on the mountain, the fire burned.

'Dad!' Still frantic with worry about their dolphins, Fleur saw him sprinting towards them. Her heart lurched and she started to run to meet him.

Alfie tore his gaze away from the sea. Stormy, Jazz and Pearl hadn't resurfaced and there was no sign of the shark either. With no way of knowing if their dolphins were safe, he was forced to turn and follow Fleur.

'Mum! Mia!' Fleur gave a second cry as they jumped down from the headland.

James opened his arms wide and waited for Fleur to reach him. 'You're both safe – thank God for that!'

Katie ran to Alfie and held him close. 'What happened?' she asked, hugging him so hard that she squeezed the breath out of him.

'Let go and I'll tell you,' he gasped.

'The monkeys came,' Fleur began.

'They were nicking our food,' Alfie went on.

'We were at Lookout Point.'

'One of them grabbed the canvas.'

'And threw it on to the campfire.'

'Stop, stop!' James begged. 'Slow down. One at a time.'

Fleur swallowed hard then spoke more carefully. 'The canvas sent flames shooting up and they set fire to everything.'

145

'Everything?' Katie echoed. The desperate looks on Alfie and Fleur's faces told her all she needed to know. 'No – don't tell me. We've lost our shelter.'

They nodded. Mia began to cry softly.

'What about *Sandpiper*?' James asked.

'That's gone too,' Alfie confirmed. 'And the boat. And all our clothes, and the map, our beds, our hammocks ...'

'Sshhh,' Katie said, glancing at James then up at the fire on the hillside. She crouched down to comfort Mia. 'Sshh, don't cry.'

Seeing Mia in floods of tears set Fleur and Alfie off too. 'We're really sorry,' Alfie mumbled as he wiped his face with the back of his hand and tried to pretend he wasn't crying. 'We were too far away to stop it.'

James shook his head. 'It's not your fault.'

'... Monkey,' Mia cried through her tears.

'Yes, it was the monkeys' fault,' Katie murmured. She gently pushed Mia's hair back from her face then hugged her.

'No, not monkeys – Monkey,' Mia sobbed.

Fleur felt that her heart would break in two. 'She means Monkey – her Monkey.'

'Ah.' Katie rested Mia's head against her shoulder and stroked it. 'Don't cry, Mi-mi. It can't be helped.'

'Nothing can be helped,' James said, standing between Alfie and Fleur as they watched the fire creep towards the forest. 'It's out of our hands. All we can do now is watch and pray.'

Chapter Eleven

For a while the force of the fire kept the Fishers rooted to the spot. They stood mesmerized. From the beach they could see how the swirling wind drove the orange flames first this way then that, halting them in one direction before making them leap and dance in another.

'Please don't let the fire reach the forest,' Fleur whispered. Thick black smoke blocked their view of the trees so she imagined how the animals must already be breathing it into their lungs. Sooner or later it would choke them and they would have to break cover. But where would they flee? Nowhere on the island was safe now that the fire had run so completely out of control.

'We can't just stand here and do nothing,' Alfie decided as the wind changed again and smoke billowed down the hillside towards the cliff.

'What do you suggest?' The main thing on Katie's mind was that they must stick together from now on. 'Whatever we do, it has to include everyone.'

'It does. Fleur and I found a new way to get down the cliff.'

'What's wrong with our old path?' Mia asked.

The old path got cut off by the fire, but we can use this new way to climb to Lookout Point and get a better view of what's happening.'

'We already know what's happening,' James said with a weary sigh. 'I don't see the point.'

'No – I agree with Alfie,' Katie argued. 'It's better to be on the move than to stay here and feel useless. If we all stick together, we should be safe enough.'

'Me too,' Fleur added. 'I vote we climb up. That way we can be close by if any of the animals get injured and need our help.'

James was overruled and it was settled – they would all climb to the lookout.

Fleur found footholds to pick her way up the cliff, trying not to breathe in too much smoke and taking care to press her body against the rock whenever glowing sparks and flakes of hot ash gusted in their direction. James, Mia and Katie followed her, with Alfie bringing up the rear.

Every so often Fleur called out instructions. 'Watch your step, everyone; it gets a bit steeper here,' or 'There's a good foothold to the left of this next overhang.' She craned her neck and squinted through the smoke, trying to work out their best route.

'Are you OK, Mia?' Alfie called from down below.

'Yes,' came the confident reply as Mia climbed nimbly as usual and overtook both her mum and dad.

'Almost there,' Fleur told her. 'Hang on, Mi-mi – let me go first.'

Just then, a blast of hot air and an extra-thick pall of dark grey smoke swept down the mountainside. The smoke stung their eyes and made it hard to breathe.

'This had better be worth it.' James coughed to clear his lungs once it had lifted.

'This is it – we're here!' Fleur hauled herself up on to the long, wide ledge where their lookout fire had burned down to nothing. She offered Mia her hand and raised her up. With strenuous grunts and groans, James followed and then Katie. Last of all, Alfie clambered on to the ledge.

From their new vantage point everyone could see just how close to the edge of the forest the fire was and it struck fresh fear into their hearts.

'There's no way to stop it,' Alfie realized all over again. He judged that the distance between the flames and the trees was less than a hundred metres.

Fleur bit her lip and looked up through a shimmering haze of smoke towards the sky. Her eyes were still stinging and everything was blurred, but after she'd wiped them she was able to see that a bank of clouds had formed to the north and seemed to be heading towards the island. She didn't say anything to the others, but the sight gave her something to cling on to – a tiny reason to hope.

'Oh, look, everyone!' Mia's cry made them all focus on what was happening closer to home, on the scorched hillside above.

From the dark shadows of the forest, creatures began to emerge, a few at a time at first but soon building up until the whole mountainside seemed to be alive. The monkeys came first – dozens of them, racing from the tangled undergrowth and scattering in all directions. There were mothers with babies clinging to their backs, males leading groups of females, youngsters tumbling and screeching as they fled the smoke and flames. Then the tree kangaroos appeared, thumping their long, thick tails on the ground and making their bewildered, earth-bound escape. Lizards ran in amongst them – squat grey skinks, multicoloured chameleons and green geckos darting across the hillside and disappearing over a ridge to the south. Sugar gliders soared through the smoke-filled air with bats, parrots and mynah birds. Rats raced out into the open with wild boars stampeding after them, fleeing for their lives.

Six of the monkeys fled straight past Lookout Point, down the cliff on to the beach where they raced headlong for the rocks. Families of boars rushed more clumsily down the hill and veered off towards the southern ridge, snorting as they went. One was limping and trailed behind the rest, but soon he too stumbled out of sight.

'Oh, poor things.' Fleur could hardly bear to watch the flight from the forest. There was panic everywhere as flames roared still closer to the trees and smoke billowed in every direction.

Alfie looked up as dozens of fruit bats flew overhead. The nocturnal creatures had been forced out into the sunlight and flitted haphazardly through the air, flapping their leathery wings in their frantic search for safety. The sky above was grey. Clouds were drifting in front of the sun. He glanced at Fleur and noticed that she'd seen them too.

'Is that smoke in the distance?' he asked in a low voice.

She shook her head and showed him that her fingers were already tightly crossed. 'No. Those are storm clouds.' She grew certain that they were the type that usually gathered on the eastern horizon, far out to sea. Today they were rolling in from the north, about to collide with the mountain and send rain pouring down on to Dolphin Island.

'What are you two whispering about?' Mia wanted to know.

'Nothing.' It was too soon to say anything. Perhaps

the wind would switch again and send the clouds scudding clear of the island.

Meanwhile, the flight from the forest went on. Two more terrified macaques scrambled down the slope and passed close to Lookout Point. They paused to glance back at the plumes of smoke and roaring flames then took flight again. Before long they'd joined the group gathered on the headland.

'Are you hoping the same thing as me?' Alfie asked Fleur, once they were sure that the monkeys were safe. He looked up towards the storm clouds. 'That it's going to rain?'

She nodded.

'Am I wrong, or has the wind changed?' At the far end of the ledge, James had noticed that the smoke no longer whirled wildly across the hillside.

'Yes, it's more settled.' Katie's hopes revived when she saw that the fire was now being held back. It still burned strongly but its progress towards the forest was slower than before. 'The problem is, now it's blowing the smoke right in our faces.'

It was true. Thick blue smoke billowed down the

slope towards the ledge, forcing them to take cover under the overhang where the air was easier to breathe.

'I'm going to take another look.' After a minute or two Fleur took a deep breath then covered her mouth and nose with her hand. She darted back out on to the ledge and stared up at the fire-ravaged mountain. Yes, the wildfire had definitely slowed down and now blue-black storm clouds hung low over the jagged peak. She gasped as she felt the first cold splashes of rain on her forehead and cheeks.

Alfie joined her. He held out his hand to watch the heavy drops fall on to his palm.

Then, as Alfie and Fleur stood out in the open, the clouds suddenly burst. It rained like it had never rained before, drenching the island in a torrential downpour. It lashed down and soaked the scorched earth, attacking the deadly wildfire that had threatened to destroy everything in its path. The flames hissed, fought back, spurted upwards in angry yellow bursts, hissed again then died. Muddy rivulets ran down the mountainside. Smoke thinned and dispersed as the relentless, life-saving rain continued to fall.

*

After the storm, there was silence. The air cleared and the sky turned blue. A golden sun was sinking in the west.

'Shall we see if we can use the old path to go down to the beach?' James asked once the rain had stopped. 'We need to go back to base camp before dark and see if there's anything we can salvage.'

It was Alfie's turn to lead the way. He strode down the blackened hillside towards Butterfly Falls, testing the ground as he went. 'It's OK so far,' he called back. 'The rain's cooled everything down. It's safe to walk here.'

Fleur caught him up as he reached the waterfall. 'I'm not looking forward to this,' she admitted.

'Me neither. We'll be upset, for sure.' He crouched by the water, cupped his hands and scooped up water to drink.

The storm had filled the stream to overflowing and now it cascaded noisily over the rocks, finding new ways on to the rocks below. 'All that work.' Fleur remembered all too well how long it had taken them to make the shelter out of wood, bamboo and palm leaves.

'We were really proud of it when we'd finished. Now it'll take for ever to rebuild.'

'It's the stuff we salvaged from *Merlin* that I mind most about.' Alfie thought of the guts it had taken for them to paddle their first flimsy raft out there and rescue as much as they could before the yacht had sunk – knives and plates, part of the sail, a hammock for their injured dad. He still had nightmares about watching waves crash against the shattered hull and water flood into the cabins while Fleur had gathered what she could.

'Now we have to start all over again – the shelter, the food store, the raft …' It was a grim prospect but Fleur knew they had no choice. It was the only way for them to survive.

'Don't look so down in the dumps, you two.' James had arrived at the waterfall ahead of Mia and Katie. 'I know what you're thinking: that we've lost everything and we'll have to start all over again.'

'Wow, Dad – you must be a mind-reader.' Alfie made a feeble attempt to make a joke.

James smiled. 'Look at it this way – at least now we

know what we're doing. The first time around, none of us had a clue.'

'Yeah, the roof of the shelter leaked,' Alfie recalled with an embarrassed grin.

'We got eaten alive by insects,' Fleur reminded them. 'That was because we didn't raise the beds high enough off the ground.'

'And we kept food inside the shelter.' That had been a bad mistake because it had attracted rats.

'See?' James said. 'We've learned our lessons the hard way.'

Revived by their dad's pep talk, Alfie and Fleur gave him a high-five then went on again.

'Dad didn't mention the best thing about today,' Fleur pointed out as they set foot on the beach and stepped gingerly through the burnt-out remains of their base camp.

Alfie took in the ruins – the heap of ash that had once been their home, the charred remains of *Sandpiper* and the dugout canoe that they'd hardly started. 'What's that?'

'The animals,' she explained. 'None of them got

hurt.' Deep down this was the thing *she* cared most about. Shelters, boats and rafts could be rebuilt but lives, once taken by the flames, could never be given back.

Alfie looked away, afraid to voice the rest of what he was thinking. He took a few steps across the sand, hoping that Fleur wouldn't follow.

She ran to catch up with him. 'Why aren't you pleased?' she demanded. 'I'm right, aren't I? The monkeys, the geckos, the wild boars – they're all fine.' Even the Creature in the forest had survived, as far as they knew.

'Yes,' he muttered, walking on.

'That's good – G-O-O-D!' she insisted, following him down to the water's edge then standing with him outside George's Cave and looking out beyond the reef.

'I know it is,' he snapped back. 'You don't have to tell me. But you said none of the animals got hurt and we don't know that for sure.'

'Yes, we do.' They'd seen it with their own eyes – the wildfire had died down before it reached the trees, which proved she was right. She glanced at his worried face then followed the direction of his gaze.

The sea was calm after the storm. The waves sparkled and danced in the evening sun.

'Oh!' Fleur gasped with dawning realization. The scene was perfect, except that one thing was missing. Three things, actually. 'It's not just the animals on the mountain you're talking about, is it?'

'No.' Alfie shook his head. He searched the bay in vain.

'It's Jazz, Stormy and Pearl,' Fleur murmured. Her heart thudded inside her chest.

Last seen playing a game of dare with the tiger shark, their dolphins had been risking their lives to save them.

'Now do you get it?' Alfie asked, his eyes narrowed and fixed on the horizon. He vowed to himself that he wouldn't move from here. He would stand by the shore until it grew dark, waiting, watching and hoping with all his heart for them to return to Base Camp Bay.

Chapter Twelve

'Three kitchen knives, two pewter plates and a tin mug.' At daybreak next morning, James carefully laid out the items that they'd rescued from the fire so far.

As soon as it was light, the family had started to rake through the ashes of their shelter for a second time. They'd carried out their first search at dusk then given up and spent the night huddled together for warmth in George's Cave. No one had slept.

'I'm cold.' Mia's quavering voice had punctuated the hours of darkness. 'My tummy hurts. I'm hungry.'

During the long, sleepless hours, Alfie had thought only of Pearl and how much she meant to him. Pearl was the reason he was still alive. She'd saved him when *Merlin* capsized and had guided him through the storm to the safety of the nearest shore. Likewise, Jazz and Stormy had been there for Fleur and Mia. The dolphins had saved them. *We'd never have done it without you*, he'd thought. *We need you again. Please come back.*

'It's hardly anything.' Mia said what everyone was thinking as the sun rose now over the horizon and they stared at the measly collection of salvaged objects.

Every single thing that had made life comfortable on Dolphin Island – their sunhats and spare clothes, the life-jackets that they'd used as pillows, their straw mattresses – had gone up in flames.

'It's better than nothing,' Katie insisted.

James agreed. 'We're down but not out. We have to pick ourselves up and make the best of things.'

Alfie took the hint and carried on searching. He stooped to pick up a small, round object and brush away the grey ash. It was the watch that had once belonged to one of the sailors on *Kestrel*. The strap was missing and the glass was cracked. He held it up to his ear then threw it down again with a frown. 'No good – not working.'

Fleur used a sturdy stick to rummage through the

mess. She soon came across two of the bone blades that Alfie had carved, wiped them on her shorts then added them to the short row of items laid out on a flat rock.

Alfie saw the blades and grinned. 'Hang on a second – I've found something else.' He had stubbed his toe on the corner of a hard square object buried deep in the ashes. He dug down and pulled out a large metal box.

'What is it?' Mia helped him to dust it down.

He recognized the white cross on the scorched red lid. 'Cool – it's our first-aid box.'

'Here – let's see if there's anything we can still make use of.' James took the box from him and looked inside.

'Yuck!' Mia pulled a face. A tube of white antiseptic cream had melted in the heat of the fire and spread all over the bandages and sticking plasters.

'Wait.' Alfie retrieved a small pair of scissors from the sticky mess, followed by a bottle of sunscreen. 'These seem OK.'

'Put them with the rest of the stuff,' James said while Fleur dipped her fingers into the spilt cream then dabbed it on to the graze on her elbow. It was sore to the touch but the antiseptic cream would help to make it better.

Three kitchen knives, two plates, a tin mug, two bone blades, a metal box, a pair of first-aid scissors and a bottle of sunscreen. Alfie shook his head at the sheer scale of the task ahead.

'I know,' Fleur said quietly while the others carried on searching. 'It really isn't much to start over with, is it?'

'Maybe we should go back to the wreck and fetch that old rope and the pieces of canvas.'

'And the wooden chest.' *That's all very well*, she thought. *But what if the viper is still there?*

'The big question is – do we rebuild the shelter here or do we relocate?' Katie tried to raise everyone's spirits by looking to the future. 'After all, you know what they say – location is everything when you're choosing somewhere to live!'

'I vote we stay here.' James was the first to speak. 'It's handy for Butterfly Falls, which is our main water supply.'

'But the palm trees won't shade us from the sun any

165

more.' Fleur pointed to the bare, blackened columns towering over them. 'Anyway, it's too sad to remember what base camp used to be like,' she added.

'How about moving to Turtle Beach?' Alfie was quick to see reasons to build in the neighbouring bay. 'The fire didn't spread in that direction so there are still plenty of bamboo canes to make our shelter. It'll save having to carry them over the headland. Plus, we've still got a stash of canvas hidden away. We can use that for the roof.'

'That makes sense. Good thinking, you two.' Katie nodded and smiled.

Their mum's praise gave them a boost. 'There are palm trees for shade,' Fleur reminded everyone. 'Plus sugarcane and yuccas.'

The mention of food made Mia remember that she was hungry. She went to what was left of their old food store and pulled out two scorched coconuts. 'Is this all there is for breakfast?'

'Yes, and we're lucky we've got those.' Alfie used a knife to pierce holes in the shells. Then he poured the milk into the metal cup and handed it to Mia who drank greedily.

'Remember, Mi-mi? This is what it was like when we first got here.' Fleur picked up a heavy stone and used it to crack open the first shell. Alfie scooped out the white flesh with his knife and handed Mia a chunk. 'We only had coconut to eat. That was before we learned how to catch fish.'

Mia nodded and answered with her mouth full. 'And find birds' eggs on the cliff and jackfruit in the trees at the edge of the forest,' she mumbled.

'It was even before we learned how to build a fire.' Katie dipped into her pocket and took out the lens that Mia had found in Pirate Cave. 'I told you this would come in handy, didn't I?'

'That's our next job then,' James interrupted briskly. 'Kids, you stay here and chill while your mum and I climb up to Lookout Point and try to relight the fire with the lens from the glasses that Mia found. We won't be long, touch wood.'

'Go for a swim if you like,' Katie suggested as they left base camp.

'Yay – swim!' Mia didn't need telling twice. She shot

off down the beach towards the sea.

'Uh-oh.' Alfie grimaced then shot Fleur an anxious look. 'Why didn't we tell them about the shark?'

'There was too much going on. We didn't get the chance.' She set off after Mia and soon caught up with her. 'Actually, we can't go into the water,' she told her awkwardly.

Mia's face fell. 'Why not?'

'Because of the shark.' Fleur made her wait for Alfie to join them. 'I know – I've got a different idea. The tide's coming in. Why don't we build a sandcastle with a moat then watch the waves knock it down?'

'OK.' Pleased by the notion, Mia remembered a plank of wood that she'd found on the beach. Thinking it might be useful, she'd stored it safely on a ledge in the cave, along with her collection of shells. 'I'll fetch something to dig with,' she told Alfie and Fleur as she dashed away again.

Alfie waited at the water's edge with a frown on his face. 'We have to tell Mum and Dad when they get back,' he insisted. 'They need to know it's not safe to go swimming.'

'Let's wait,' she pleaded. Somehow telling James and Katie about the shark's surprise visit would make it seem even more real and terrifying.

He watched a small wave roll in and break against his ankles. Feeling the undertow shift the sand beneath his feet, he changed the subject. 'What if they don't come back?' he asked quietly.

He didn't have to say their names – Fleur knew who he was talking about. 'They will.' She had to hold fast to the belief that she would see Jazz again.

Suddenly Mia burst out of the cave, clutching her precious Monkey to her chest. 'I found him! I found him!'

'Where?' Fleur wanted to know.

'I forgot – he wasn't in the shelter. I put him on the ledge with my piece of wood. Look – I found Monkey!'

'Wow, that's brilliant.' Alfie meant what he said. Mia had owned the stuffed toy since she was two and she still took him to bed with her. His brown fur was worn bare in patches and he had one eye missing, but she didn't care.

Mia was so delighted that she forgot all about the

sandcastle and pranced along the shore. 'Guess what, Monkey – we have to build a new shelter 'cos the other one burned down. We have to start the raft and the canoe all over again ...'

Her voice faded as she climbed the headland that separated Base Camp Beach from Turtle Beach.

'I'm glad someone's happy,' Fleur said with a long sigh. She closed her eyes and felt the warmth of the sun on her face.

Alfie bit his lip and stared out to sea as if by looking long enough he could perform magic and make Pearl, Jazz and Stormy appear. But it was no good – there were no dolphins to be seen.

'Yay!'

Mia's distant shout made Fleur open her eyes. 'What now?'

'Come and look!' Mia waved at them and held Monkey aloft. 'Hurry up, come quick!'

'Shall we?' Fleur asked.

'I guess we'd better,' Alfie decided.

With Mia's excited yells disturbing the peace, they set off along the sand.

'Faster!' Mia demanded. She beckoned again then jumped out of sight down the far side of the rocks.

Fleur and Alfie picked up speed. 'Maybe she's seen some turtles,' he suggested.

'Yeah – that'd be cool.' Fleur broke into a jog that soon turned into a run.

Before long they both reached the rocks and began to climb.

'This had better be something good,' Alfie grumbled. 'Not just the usual heap of old junk that the waves have thrown up.'

They scrambled to the top and looked down on to the next beach. 'OK, Mia – why are we here?' Fleur called.

Instead of answering, she danced on the spot and pointed towards the sea.

At first Fleur and Alfie were dazzled by the sun in the east. They had to shade their eyes with both hands.

'This is where we really need sunglasses,' Fleur complained. Then she gasped and grabbed Alfie's arm. 'Do you see what I see?'

He couldn't miss them. There they were, fifty

metres out, sleek grey bodies glistening in the sun, twisting and rolling and lazily flicking their tail flukes – Jazz, Pearl and Stormy. They whistled their signature tunes – a long, shrill, single-note call from Stormy, a high-low from Jazz and Pearl's songbird chirrups.

'See!' Mia shrieked as, still clutching Monkey, she ran into the sea. 'Our dolphins came to see us on our new beach!'

Fleur and Alfie couldn't speak – it was beyond words. Instead, they ran to the furthest point of the headland and dived into the deep water.

They came up surrounded by clouds of bright bubbles, face to face with Jazz and Pearl.

'You're here!' Fleur cried, throwing her arms around Jazz and allowing herself to be towed gently through the water.

'You came back.' Alfie looked into Pearl's eyes and stroked her head. Now he believed in magic.

Stormy swam up to Mia and waited for her to climb on his back. Then he set off with her across the bay. 'Yay!' she yelled, holding his fin with one hand as she held Monkey high in the air.

The race was on. Pearl held steady as Alfie sat astride then she set off after Mia and Stormy. She cut cleanly through the water until she drew level with the leaders. 'Come on, slowcoaches!' he yelled at Fleur and Jazz.

'OK, let's show them.' Fleur slid her leg over Jazz's back and held tight to his fin. The shark had moved on. The dolphins were out of danger and now everything – *everything* – would be fine. 'I'm ready,' she murmured.

With a sideways flick of his broad tail flukes, Jazz gave chase. He carried Fleur through the cold, clear waves – away from Dolphin Island, far out to sea.

The story
continues
in ...

DOLPHIN
ISLAND

Missing

Read on for
a sneak peek ...

Chapter One

Mia Fisher sat by the campfire in Base Camp Bay smiling from ear to ear.

"'Happy birthday to you!'" Her brother, Alfie, and sister, Fleur, yelled out the words. "'Happy birthday, dear Mi-mi, happy birthday to you!'"

The sun was sinking in a vivid orange sky – Mia's favourite colour. It made the waves dance and sparkle and lit up the happy face of the birthday girl.

'Happy birthday, honey-bunch.' Mia's dad, James, gave her a big bear hug then swung her round until she was dizzy.

'Whoa!' she gasped. Her hazel eyes were alive with happiness and wisps of brown hair, lightened by the sun after more than forty days on Dolphin Island, stuck to her hot cheeks.

Her mum Katie took her by the shoulders and steadied her. 'Seven years old today. Who'd have dreamed you'd be spending your birthday surrounded by palm trees and white sands?' A wistful look passed across her suntanned face as she squeezed Mia's hand. 'We all thought we'd be back in old England in the rain and cold.'

'Stuck in a classroom behind a boring old desk,' Alfie said with an exaggerated frown.

'Stacking the dishwasher and tidying our rooms,' thirteen-year-old Fleur added. 'Instead, here we are!' She pointed to the cliff behind them rising to Lookout Point and the tree-covered mountain beyond. Then she swept her arm towards the azure sea with its dancing waves breaking against the reef at the edge of the bay.

'We're in the middle of the South Pacific, miles from anywhere.' Alfie threw fresh wood on to the fire and watched the sparks fly upwards. 'Doing what we like when we like – beachcombing and building stuff ...'

Mia's head had stopped spinning so she skipped down the beach a little way then turned to face him.

'... Like shelters?'

'Yes, building shelters and keeping the fires going, making a dugout canoe ...'

'... Swimming with dolphins!' Mia interrupted again as she ran on towards the sea.

'Where?' Fleur sprinted after her, scanning the ocean for the first signs of Jazz, Stormy and Pearl, their fantastic dolphin friends. Alfie threw another branch on to the fire then followed them.

Mia stopped at the water's edge. 'Nowhere. I'm just saying what my favourite thing about the island is – swimming with Stormy and playing games with him.'

'Oh.' Fleur turned down the corners of her mouth. 'I thought you'd spotted them swimming this way.' She saw a white heron rise from the dark reef and flap towards Turtle Beach headland where small storm petrels waded in shallow rock pools searching for crabs. But there were no telltale fins rising to the surface, no shiny domed heads and sleek grey bodies entering the bay. Fleur quickly got over her disappointment. 'Anyway, Mi-mi, you left the party early. Alfie hasn't had time to give you your present yet.'

'Ooh, what is it?' Mia clapped her hands.

'It's … hey, watch out!' Alfie warned as she turned her back on the incoming tide. A large wave hit her from behind, sweeping her off her feet.

Fleur and Alfie rushed to drag the birthday girl on to dry land. Fleur rescued Mia's straw hat floating in the water then jammed it on her head.

'I'm going back to base camp for Alfie's present,' Mia reminded them. She marched, sopping wet, towards where the fire burned brightly in the shadow of the overhanging cliff.

Halfway up the beach, Alfie caught up with her and delved into the pocket of his red shorts. 'Here – I brought it with me. I haven't had much time to make this for you. I hope it's OK.' Shyly he handed her a small object carefully wrapped in a shiny green leaf.

Mia shook water from the brim of her hat then took the gift. 'Do you know what it is, Fleur?' she asked as she turned it over and started to unwrap it.

'Yes, I saw him making it.' Fleur knew Mia would be thrilled. Alfie was clever with his hands and he'd used his special knife to carve the present, sitting cross-legged on Echo Cave Beach, where he was sure Mia wouldn't find him.

Mia's fingers fumbled with the piece of blue string that Alfie had used to keep the wrapping in place. Then she took out a softly shining, flat object and held it up to the firelight. 'It's a tiny dolphin!' she murmured. Alfie had carved it out of a piece of mother-of-pearl. It was about four centimetres long and hanging from another length of thin blue string.

'I made you a lucky charm,' Alfie explained nervously. He couldn't tell from Mia's face whether or not she liked it. In fact, from where he stood, it looked as if she was about to cry.

Tears welled up in Mia's eyes as she turned the carved dolphin this way and that. It glowed a creamy colour, with glints of pink and pale blue. Her bottom lip trembled.

'Don't be upset,' he pleaded with a worried look. 'If you don't like it, I can make you something else.'

She clasped the dolphin in the palm of her hand. 'No – I love it,' she whispered. 'These are happy tears.'

'See – she loves it,' Fleur echoed. She felt that Alfie's

gift put her own birthday present to shame. It was a fan made from bird of paradise and cockatoo feathers, hastily put together earlier that day, in between fetching water from Butterfly Falls and throwing logs on to the lookout fire. 'Alfie's present is for good luck, Mi-mi. You have to keep it with you wherever you go.'

'For ever and ever,' Mia promised as she wiped away her tears. 'Please will you tie it around my neck?' she asked Fleur.

'Now who wants a birthday pudding made out of mashed-up jackfruit and sugarcane?' Katie called.

'Me! Me! Me!' Three voices shouted as one.

'And who wants to play pass the parcel?' James asked.

'We all do!' Fleur yelled. She looked forward to a fun evening – munching gooey treats, playing party games, singing and dancing as the sun sank below the watery horizon like a burning disc of gold. Even though their last shelter had burned down in the Big Fire that had rampaged across the island only four days earlier and they'd had to start building everything all over again, the Fishers were determined to give the youngest member of their family the best birthday party ever.

The sun had gone down and the moon and stars shone in a clear sky. Fleur's stomach was full as she strolled down to the shore, leaving Mia already fast asleep in George's Cave. By the light of the moon eleven-year-old Alfie used a stone hammer and his knife to chip away at the canoe they'd started to hollow out from a tree trunk – one of the few things at base camp that had escaped the disastrous wildfire. Their dad was busy collecting stones at the foot of the cliff, planning to build a food store to keep their fish and fruit safe from marauding monkeys, while their mum had already begun her night shift at Lookout Point, keeping the fire there alive.

The sound of the ocean filled Fleur's head – the everlasting roar of breaking waves and the suck of pebbles as they ebbed. A cool breeze blew her long brown hair back from her face as she stood ankle-deep, trying to block out memories of birthdays back home – real Victoria sponge cake with jam and cream, big bowls of cheese and onion crisps, and hot dogs snugly wrapped in soft bread rolls. *With lashings of tomato ketchup,* she thought with a sigh. *So much for trying not to think about home.*

In her mind's eye she pictured the Fishers' pretty riverside house, with Gran and Granddad living next door. Home had things that she'd once taken for granted: a roof that didn't leak, proper glass windows and brick walls. A real bed with a soft mattress and a cosy duvet. A toilet that flushed, hot running water, shampoo …

'Are you OK?' Alfie had come up behind her and now spoke in a low murmur.

'Yep,' she nodded without turning her head.

'What're you thinking about?'

'Nothing.' *Scented shampoo that disappears down the plughole in a white, soapy stream, leaving your hair silky soft. Giant fluffy towels, Mia in her panda onesie, snuggling under the duvet, pleading for a bedtime story.*

'You're wishing we were at home.' Alfie bent to pick up a pebble then skimmed it across the silvery water. Four bounces then *plop* – it vanished without trace.

'How did you guess?'

'Easy-peasy.' Forty-one days stranded on a tiny island in the middle of the Pacific made everyone homesick, especially on a special occasion like a birthday. 'I always know what you're daydreaming about when you wander off by yourself.'

Fleur sighed. 'Do you think Mia had a good time today?'

'Yep.' Alfie skimmed another pebble. Six bounces then *plop*.

'She loved your lucky charm.'

'And your fan.'

'I'll make one for you if you like.' Fleur looked sideways at him and grinned.

'No thanks.' Brightly coloured feathers weren't Alfie's thing – or Fleur's. They preferred plain old palm leaf fans any day.

Together they stood for a while and gazed out to sea. Then Fleur broke the silence. 'Alfie, do you think we'll ever leave Dolphin Island?'

He didn't answer straight away. 'Yeah – once we've finished the canoe,' he said hesitantly.

'What then?' Fleur knew that it would only be big

enough for two people. 'Who'll go off in it and try to find help?'

'Mum and you maybe?'

'Or you and Dad?' Another picture came to mind of Alfie and their dad paddling off in the tiny canoe, out on to the big ocean, heading south towards Misty Island. Waves and wind, thunder and lightning, danger all around; Fleur's unruly thoughts made her shiver.

Alfie shrugged. 'Anyway, the canoe is nowhere near finished so we're stuck here for a bit longer. And there's still lots to do.'

He and Fleur turned away from the water. They walked up the beach towards the cave where Mia lay on her new sleeping platform with Monkey, her bedraggled soft toy. Fleur's pet gecko, George, kept watch from his ledge, occasionally flicking out his long tongue to catch spiders. Beyond the cave they crossed another stretch of white sand then skirted wide of the campfire to approach the bushes and palm trees growing at the base of the cliff.

'Lots to do.' Fleur echoed Alfie's words as she came close to the burnt-out shell of their old shelter. The fire started by the macaque monkeys had left hardly anything untouched. Flames had destroyed the thatched roof and the walls made from panels of woven palm fronds. Practically every single thing they owned, apart from a few metal objects like knives and pans, had collapsed into a heap of grey ashes. Gone was their map of the island painstakingly drawn on to a scrap of sailcloth, their notched calendar stick, the clothes that they'd salvaged from sunken *Merlin* – all gone.

'But our new shelter will be bigger and better,' Alfie promised. He clenched his fist, flexed his muscles and showed her his biceps. 'Look – Superman!'

He made Fleur laugh. 'At least we know how to build one now.' They'd learned that it was best to hammer strong stakes into the ground and build a raised bamboo platform for the shelter to stand on. And now they knew which palm fronds to choose for the best weaving material. They'd learned how to lash the panels securely to upright poles so that the wind didn't blow the walls down. A watertight roof was the most important thing of all. So she, Mia and Alfie had already trawled Turtle Beach and Echo Cave Beach for suitable materials – plastic sacks, pieces of old sails – anything waterproof they could find among mounds of rubbish washed on to the shore.

Fleur stepped up on to the half-built platform, her face glowing in the firelight. 'I reckon we should head south to Pirate Cave Beach first thing tomorrow,' she suggested quietly. 'See if we can find anything useful there.'

'Yeah, like more plastic containers for collecting water. We have to replace the old ones.' Alfie knew that the route would take them past a small grove of bamboos, which always came in handy in any case.

'Early,' Fleur insisted, her mind still on the building work. 'Before it gets too hot.' Bigger and better – a shelter built of driftwood and bamboo canes, palm fronds and grasses, with stone steps leading up to the front door, an awning to provide shade and a separate, stone-built food store that the monkeys couldn't raid.

'Deal,' Alfie agreed. He fed the campfire then yawned. 'I bet I'll be awake before you.'

'No you won't.' Fleur jumped down from the platform on to the sand then strode off towards their temporary sleeping quarters in George's Cave. 'You'll still be snoring when I'm up and dressed.'

He overtook her at a slow jog. 'How much do you bet?'

'One conch shell and two cockatoo feathers.'

'Deal,' he said again, bumping knuckles with Fleur as he tiptoed into the cave.

More adventures on Dolphin Island

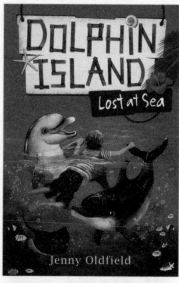

Six books to collect!